"I'm going to bring Troy to live with me. Ray said you'd help me."

Elle stopped and spun around. "Are you serious?" She didn't know whether to applaud his decision or be worried for Troy's welfare.

"Dead serious." He glanced around to where Troy squirmed under the covers. "Will you help?"

Elle bit her lip and reluctantly nodded. For Troy's sake she'd help Max. She really had no choice if Ray had already committed her.

"I'll talk to Ray. We'll put together a plan. But first I need to go home to shower and change."

"You can do that here," he insisted. "I'm sure I can find something for you to wear."

"No, thank you." She continued on her journey toward freedom.

His hand wrapped around hers derailing her escape.

"Max! Stop it." She pushed at his shoulders. "Are you insane?"

"I was hoping to change your mind about leaving."

"Well, you haven't." She tried to step back, but his arms tightened as he stared into her eyes.

"Come on, Elle, we both know the animosity between us is a defense against an inconvenient attraction."

"I know nothing of the kind."

She refused to accept that the sizzle between them held any depth. Even if she agreed with him, there were too many complications for them ever to consider acting on a mutual attraction.

BABY UNDER THE CHRISTMAS TREE

BY
TERESA CARPENTER

First published in Great Britain 2012
by Mills & Boon, an imprint of Harlequin (UK) Limited.
Harlequin (UK) Limited, Eton House, 18-24 Paradise Road,
Richmond, Surrey TW9 1SR

© Teresa Carpenter 2012

ISBN: 978 0 263 22849 6

Harlequin (UK) policy is to use papers that are natural, renewable and recyclable products and made from wood grown in sustainable forests. The logging and manufacturing process conform to the legal environmental regulations of the country of origin.

Printed and bound in Great Britain
by CPI Antony Rowe, Chippenham, Wiltshire

Teresa Carpenter believes in the power of unconditional love, and that there's no better place to find it than between the pages of a romance novel. Reading is a passion for Teresa—a passion that led to a calling. She began writing more than twenty years ago, and marks the sale of her first book as one of her happiest memories. Teresa gives back to her craft by volunteering her time to Romance Writers of America on a local and national level.

A fifth generation Californian, she lives in San Diego, within miles of her extensive family, and knows that with their help she can accomplish anything. She takes particular joy and pride in her nieces and nephews, who are all bright, fit, shining stars of the future. If she's not at a family event you'll usually find her at home—reading, writing, or playing with her adopted Chihuahua, Jefe.

'Teresa Carpenter's HER BABY, HIS PROPOSAL
makes an oft-used premise work brilliantly
through skilled plotting, deft characterisation
and just the right amount of humour.'
—*RT Book Reviews*

Recent books by Teresa Carpenter:

THE SHERIFF'S DOORSTEP BABY
THE PLAYBOY'S GIFT
SHERIFF NEEDS A NANNY
THE BOSS'S SURPRISE SON

For RWA San Diego,
the best RWA chapter in the world.
Now 30 years strong.
For all the members past and present
who have helped me to get where I am today.
Thank you for being my friends, my colleagues,
my fans. The journey isn't over yet.

PROLOGUE

ELLE AUSTIN SAT very still in the corner of her bunk, knees tucked up to her chest under the yellow satin of her Belle princess dress. Retreating from the chaos reigning in the room, she smoothed her hand over the soft material. She loved her Belle dress.

Mama had made the gown just for her and she liked it better than the costume that came with her admission to Princess Camp. Mostly because Mama didn't do anything girlie, but when her parents had agreed to let Elle come to camp, Mama took a class and made the dress. Elle figured Mama got a lot of help from the teacher, but she didn't care. Her Belle dress shimmered and flowed and was the most beautiful in camp. Everyone said so.

"What's wrong, Elle?" Amanda came to sit on the edge of Elle's bed. Posture straight, hands clasped in her lap amid the full skirt of her Rapunzel dress, Amanda's serene smile brought a moment's calm to the chaotic activity dominating the cabin.

Elle wanted to cover her ears but she wasn't a baby anymore. At eleven she was big enough to come to Princess Camp alone. That meant she was big enough to handle a little friendly bustling.

"Everyone is talking at once." She forced a smile for

Amanda. "How can anyone hear what anyone else is saying?"

"With all your brothers I'd think you'd be used to a lot of noise and activity."

"I am." Elle pleated her skirt between tense fingers. She loved her family, knew they loved her, but she often felt the misfit among the athletic, boisterous crowd. She confessed to her friend something she'd never told anyone. "But I don't like it. It makes me nervous. I like order."

"Me, too." Amanda nodded. "But this is fun noise. Everyone is excited about the talent show. They're just sharing their ideas and claiming their spots."

"But no one is paying attention." Wasted noise, wasted energy, it made everything in her go tight. And her stomach hurt.

"I know." Amanda stood and wound her way through the six girls dancing and twirling in the middle of the room. At her bunk she bent and pulled a book out of her backpack. A minute later she was back and handing Elle the book, which was actually a journal, and a purple pen.

"For you. To take down what everyone is saying. My grandmother says organization is the foundation of greatness. And my grandfather says chaos is merely random patterns that need to be put in order."

"I can take notes." Elle sat forward and took the book. She didn't really want to try to make sense of the excited chatter, but it had to be better than hiding in the corner. Amanda and Michelle were so pretty and so smart. Elle refused to be a sissy baby in front of them.

She nodded and began to listen for the different voices, pulling individuals out of the mix. Michelle first; her melodic voice made her easy to discern.

Elle noted her friend's choice of singing a song from *Sleeping Beauty.* Of course.

Next the Little Mermaid twins were enthusing together about a tap-dance routine.

Cinderella wanted to talk costumes.

And Mulan did a kick as she announced she'd be doing martial arts.

Elle bent over the pad, quickly taking down all the ideas she heard. Soon she had lots of notes and her stomach didn't hurt anymore. No longer curled into the corner, she sat on the edge of the bed directing the action as a plan began to emerge.

Elle liked plans.

Amanda smiled and Elle grinned back, happy to have order restored.

CHAPTER ONE

THE RING OF THE PHONE made Elle sit straight up in bed. Blinking, she glanced at the clock. Twenty till two in the morning. Family or work? At this hour neither was good.

Still she prayed for work as she flipped on the light and reached for her cell phone. Usually that only meant a trip downtown to a bail bondsman, not large-scale injuries, which were the only reason family would be calling.

She scanned for caller ID but it was an unknown number. No clue there.

"Hello," she said briskly, cringing when her voice came out sleep-husky instead.

"Ellie," a deep voice drawled, relieving her of worry over family, and swinging all that anxiety over to annoyance at the caller. "I hope I woke you and didn't catch you in the middle of something more interesting."

"Maxwell." Of course. Max "The Beast" Beasley, enforcer for the San Diego Thunder hockey team and her personal nemesis. And a man who had no right to question her nighttime activities. "I suppose this means you're in jail?"

"Me and a few of the guys. We went out for drinks to celebrate Jaden's twenty-first birthday. It got a little out of hand."

"Is anyone hurt?"

"Babe, define hurt. We take a bigger beating on the ice."

"Don't call me babe. Or Ellie. My name is Elle. Or Ms. Austin to you."

"So harsh," he idly rebuked her. "Maybe you need something interesting going at two in the morning to loosen you up a little."

That stung.

"Careful, Maxwell, or the only thing you'll be cozying up to tonight is your cell mate."

"Ellie, you tease. We both know that won't happen."

She gritted her teeth as the line went dead. He was right of course. This was part of her job, the annoying part. Being Deputy Public Relations Director meant she got the late-night calls when the players played hard in public and needed bailing out of trouble.

She might wish Max Beasley would be traded to some Siberian league, but if she wanted her boss's job when he retired next year, she needed to keep The Beast happy.

She threw on jeans, a purple sweater and flat-heeled boots. After sweeping her dark red hair into a sleek pony-tail, she put on a dusting of makeup. And then glared into her light brown eyes, disgusted with herself for primping.

There was no one to impress tonight, certainly not a six-foot-two blond with midnight-blue eyes, a dashing dimple in his right cheek and a sexy scar on his chin.

It took fifteen minutes to get from Elle's Lake Murray condo to the jail in downtown San Diego. This time of the morning she could probably do it in half that time, but preferring not to join the players behind bars, she held to the speed limit.

A complete rule breaker, Max would no doubt sneer at her judicious driving habits. Let him. After all, she was the one bailing him out of jail.

She believed in rules, lists and goals. They'd gotten her where she was. When she'd returned from Princess Camp with a new love of creating order out of chaos, she'd put her new skill to work helping her dad with his sports teams.

It came in handy at San Diego State University where, as well as being a student, she worked as assistant to the athletic director. Part of the job included being the public-relations liaison for all the different sports. She was responsible for coordinating efforts and maximizing promotional opportunities.

She made great contacts at State and at twenty-six she was the deputy director of public relations for a national hockey team. Well on her way to having her own PR firm by the time she turned thirty-five.

She parked on the street across from Smart Bail Bonds and Harry Smart stepped out to meet her.

"Ms. Austin." He greeted her with a gap-toothed smile. Shorter than average with a round belly covered by a Hawaiian shirt, he had thinning brown hair and a pleasant disposition. He always insisted on walking her to the jail adjacent to the San Diego County Courthouse. "It's been a while since the boys caused a ruckus. They must be missing their captain. I heard Ian is going to be out for eight weeks."

"That's right, but they started out strong, so we have momentum on our side." Elle forced a smile when she wanted to shake her head. She knew the rules of hockey. Thanks to her brothers she knew the rules to most sports. And it was that knowledge that had earned her a rookie position with the Thunder organization eighteen months ago. And she loved her job, even if she didn't understand the sport, the sheer violence of it.

She did know the more fights on the ice, the more fans

in the stands. The games were battles, the players modern-day gladiators: fierce, competitive, combative, and the harder they fought the more the crowd cheered.

And Maxwell "The Beast" Beasley led the pack.

He was a public-relations dream and nightmare. The public loved his bad-boy persona as long as the team was winning, but when the team took a few losses, the public had little patience for player antics.

Elle avoided the lone-wolf player as much as possible.

Through the window of the bond office she saw a few of the wives and girlfriends of the players he'd led astray tonight.

When The Beast chose to party, everyone wanted to party with him.

But it was a subdued, somewhat sheepish crew turned over to her an hour later. Usually they were still full of themselves, boasting over their deeds and conquests of the night. But there was little chatter as they walked the few blocks to the bond office.

"That's a pretty nasty cut, Hank." She eyed the goalie, who sported a crude butterfly bandage over a slash on his cheek. "You should stop at an emergency room on the way home."

"Nah." He cleared his throat. "It's just a scratch."

"Hmm." Though his was the worst, all six of the burly men showed battle scars. Her gaze skipped over Max to land on the youngest of the group. At six-six and two-twenty, Jaden was hardly a child, but his downcast eyes and hunched shoulders gave him the look of a sulky teenager. "Happy birthday, Jaden."

He shrugged. "Thanks."

"Be nice, Grier." Max cut the younger man with a cold glare. "She just bailed your butt out of jail."

"I said thanks," Jaden snarled back. A slight slur revealed that a couple of hours and a visit to the slammer hadn't cleared all the alcohol from his system. He sent Elle a sideways look. "I got your card."

She nodded. Her mother had taught her the power of the greeting card, and Elle plied it zealously. Her goal was to build up a personal connection with the players, because it made it harder for them to turn her down when she needed them for special events. Since she'd joined the team, she'd given every player a card on his birthday. Except Max.

Cringing slightly she justified the inaction by reminding herself she hadn't thought of the cards until after his birthday the first year, and last year the team had been out of town. She'd meant to give him his card; she'd just never got around to it.

And then he hadn't deserved a card.

Still, her mother would call shame on her.

"This night had bad news written all over it from the moment we arrived at the bar and saw junior here had started to party without us." A voice grumbled from the back. "Kid, you need to learn to pace yourself."

"I'm not a kid." Jaden whirled to confront the other man, momentum and unsteadiness putting him right in the defenseman's face. "I'm an adult."

"You're a punk." The defenseman brought his arm up to brush Jaden aside.

Elle cringed as she saw it developing, and sure enough Jaden pushed back and a shoving match broke out.

No time. She had no time to intervene. No time to get out of the way.

Feeling like a child among giants, Elle expected to be crushed even as she tried to scurry backward.

Suddenly a hard arm swept around her waist, and Max swung them in a one-eighty so he took the brunt of the six-foot-five, two-hundred-seventy-pound wingman smashing into them.

Protected by his bulk she had the impression of massive strength, a hard body, a whiff of spicy aftershave and a huge impact. He didn't even grunt.

But he cursed a red-white-and-blue streak after setting her safely aside and wading into the center of the fray.

"Idiots. You almost took out Elle. Get your heads straight." He gave Jaden a hard-eyed stare. "We've already put on enough of a show tonight. Get your rides and go home."

The men quickly dispersed.

Shaken, Elle straightened her jacket and brushed her hands over her hair, ensuring her sleek ponytail was intact.

Max homed in on her. "You okay?"

She shuddered under his direct regard, but lifted her chin and answered smoothly. "Of course."

His dark gaze ran over her, checking her out for himself. He nodded. "Let's go."

"My car is at the bar." Jaden managed to slur and whine at the same time. Not an easy feat.

"And you can thank your lucky ass for that. If I ever hear of you driving drunk, I'll make sure your butt rides the bench for the whole season."

"No, huh," Jaden blustered. "You don't have that kind of say-so."

"No." Max's smile held an edge of malice. "But you can't play with your leg in a cast."

Jaden paled. "Don't be joking, man. A break can end a career."

"And driving drunk can end a life. I have no problem making that decision for you."

"Gentlemen." Elle stepped forward, intent on taking

control of the situation. "It's three-fifteen in the morning. Can you put the equipment away so we can go home? One of us has to work in a few hours."

Max waved his arm in an after-you gesture. "Lead the way. You don't mind giving us a ride, right?"

"I'm going to tell coach." Jaden stomped ahead of them. Then he stopped and swung around, his unsure balance almost tripping him up. "You're my witness Ms. A. You heard him threaten me."

"No," she denied and looked both ways before crossing the street to her car. "I heard him offer you a life lesson." And, oh, how it hurt to defend the man. "If you have two licks of sense, you'll listen to him. And you'll be benched before he can ever get to you if you mention this incident to Coach."

She unlocked her red car and they all climbed in. Reaching for her seat belt, she glanced at Max and saw he had anchored himself in. She nodded when she heard Jaden's belt click and only then did she start the car.

"Drop Jaden first." Max directed her once they reached the five freeway. And then he turned to the man in the backseat. "You better tell her the rest."

Elle got a bad feeling and her gaze flicked to the rear-view mirror. Jaden was one big scowl. He muttered something under his breath.

"What?"

"I may have—" He cleared his throat. "I kind of, ah, could have—" Cough. "Thrown the first punch."

"Jaden, Jaden." She sighed as her mind raced. The news was as bad as she feared. She could only hope the damage was minimal to both man and property. "That's an automatic ten-thousand-dollar penalty."

Narrowing her eyes at Max, she reached past him for the digital recorder in the glove box. "This is your fault."

"How do you figure?" His gaze rose from her cleavage to meet her eyes. And he lifted one dark brow.

"You took him drinking."

"It wasn't only me. Plus he's his own man now. Didn't you hear him?"

She ground her teeth together. Of course he took no responsibility. She turned her attention to Jaden, demanding he tell her everything he remembered.

He protested that it had happened too fast and he didn't remember anything, but she kept after him until he told the whole story. By then they were at his place. She turned to face him before he got out.

"Tomorrow I want you to go through it again, write it down. And be in my office at ten o'clock."

He groaned but nodded, and then climbed from the car. She watched until he was safely inside.

Luckily the fifteen-minute ride from Jaden's Fashion Valley condo to Max's Mount Helix home concluded in silence. In fact, Elle thought Max had dozed off, but it appeared he had nothing more to say to her than she had to say to him because he immediately opened his eyes and reached for the door latch when she pulled into the driveway next to his vehicle.

She rolled her eyes and sighed, ready for the night to be over. The dash clock read 3:45 a.m., which meant she should make it home by four.

Max climbed from the car while she debated the merits of going back to bed against getting a jump on the Jaden issue.

"Thanks," he bent to say before slamming the door.

Yeah, right. Mr. Glib he wasn't. At least it was an acknowledgment, and considering the weariness in his voice she figured she was lucky to get that. With home in mind she put the car in Reverse and waited for Max to get to his door.

He'd barely cleared her front hood when a car lurched to a stop behind her, effectively blocking the driveway. She frowned at the rearview mirror, not at all surprised he had some young thing on call at this time of the morning.

Annoyed, Elle put the car in Park and stepped out.

"Excuse me," she said to the slim brunette who jumped out of the vehicle. "I'm leaving if you could let me out."

"Forget it," the woman snapped. "I've been waiting for hours." She pulled open the back door and bent into the car.

Elle turned to Max. "Can you tell your girlfriend to move? It's been a long night."

He flicked her an annoyed glance.

"Hey," Max called out as he walked down the drive to join Elle. "Can I help you?"

The woman reappeared, holding something she had lifted from the backseat. "This is the last time I'm doing a favor for Amber. She was supposed to be back yesterday. She gave me your info but said not to contact you. But she's not answering her phone. And neither were you." Carrying a bundled-up trench coat, she stormed up the drive and thrust the coat at Max. "I've been waiting here since one. I was about to give up and take Troy to the cops when you pulled in."

"Amber left him with you? Where's her mom?"

"Vegas. Amber can find someone else next time." She returned to the car and came back with a backpack that she pushed into Elle's arms. "I have an interview in the morning. I'm going to have rings under my eyes the size of duffel bags."

With a huff, the brunette rounded the vehicle, got behind the wheel and drove off.

Elle looked at Max. "What just happened here?"

The coat in Max's arms shifted and the material dropped to reveal a blond head of hair. Not a trench coat, but a small child.

"A baby?"

"Meet my son, Troy."

CHAPTER TWO

"YOU HAVE A CHILD?" Totally appalled, Elle stared in fascination at the boy who looked about two. He gazed from her to Max with a growing scowl. How was it possible she didn't know he had a child? "Poor kid."

"Nice." Max's frown was a near mirror of the boy's and the resemblance made her blink.

In that space of time Max turned and walked toward the house. An automatic light came on as he neared the brick pathway that led to the front door.

Elle hesitated, because really a young child in Max's care seemed such an oddity she couldn't wrap her mind around it. On the other hand, it was late and totally not her business. And given their history it would be a total mistake to get involved.

Decided, she made a move toward her car and the bulk of the boy's bag shifted in her arms.

Muttering a curse under her breath, she stomped to the front door intending to knock and hand over the backpack. But the door stood open and no one was in sight. Good. She set the backpack inside and reached for the doorknob.

A scream rang out. Followed quickly by another and another.

Elle shut the door and ran toward the sound.

Down the hall she came into the kitchen. Max stood

at a large island while Troy shrieked and tried to climb down the other side.

"He's going to fall." She raced around the island and scooped up the toddler before her prediction proved true.

Troy shrieked and struck out blindly with one bony fist.

The swing packed quite a punch and only instincts honed by being the only girl with four brothers saved her from a black eye.

"Wow. He *is* your kid, isn't he?"

The scowl on Max's face turned sharp and mean. "I don't hit women."

No. She had to admit that was one thing he'd never been accused of, and for all their differences she'd never felt physically threatened by him.

"No, but you do have a temper and you do strike out. What did you do to him?" she challenged.

"Not a damn thing. I wouldn't have let him fall," Max stated. "He's mad because he got woken up. He screams when he's tired or in a temper."

"Lovely." The boy struggled in her arms, but she murmured to him as she made her way to the sink. "Where are your glasses?"

Max pointed to a cupboard.

Filling a tumbler half-full, she offered the cup to Troy. He stopped fighting to grab the glass in two hands and drink. Finally he pushed the cup back at her and, breath hitching, demanded, "Donna!"

"Mama went bye-bye," she told him, "but Daddy's here."

"He said Donna. She's his grandmother, the one who's in Las Vegas."

Troy looked at Max, his lower lip trembled and he started to scream again. Her ears rang from the high-pitched cries.

"How long will this go on? Someone's likely to call the cops." Her boss would love that.

"Nah. The house is soundproofed."

At her bemused response, he elaborated. "I bought it that way. It cuts down on the freeway noise. And I've seen him scream like that for an hour. I've tried everything I can think of to stop him, but the truth is nothing has worked."

"What about his mother? Do you think you can find her?" She hummed softly and rocked gently back and forth, hoping the soothing actions would penetrate the boy's distress.

"Her cell is off. I left a message but if she didn't answer her friend's calls, she doesn't want to be found. Probably off with some sugar daddy. I also tagged his grandmother. Donna is the one who usually watches him. I'm sure I'll hear from her in the morning."

"Does this happen often?" How could a mother leave her kid with someone and not come home?

"A few times."

"And you're okay with that?"

An icy blue glare, sharp as his skate blades, cut her short.

"Right." She held out a hand. "Let me see your phone."

"Why?" He reached into his back pocket for his cell.

"I'm going to get the babysitter's name." She exchanged Troy for the phone and walked into the living room to make the call. She quickly accessed his call records and hit the call-back key.

A few minutes later she returned to the kitchen where Max leaned against the refrigerator and Troy sat in the middle of the island. Definitely not a happy duo.

"You owe Candi Evans a hundred dollars." She handed him his phone. "I'll email you her address."

"Was that necessary?"

"Yes. She wouldn't give me her name until I told her you wanted to express your appreciation for her bringing Troy to you. A hundred should do it."

"And we needed her data why?"

"You never know. But now we have it if we need it."

"For a hundred bucks." He scrubbed his hands over his face. "Listen, can you watch him for a few minutes?"

"You're kidding me." The man had nerve. "I have to be up in two hours. You'll probably roll out of bed around three this afternoon."

"Come on," he cajoled her. "Just long enough for me to take a shower. I want to wash the stink of the jail off."

She sighed, unable to begrudge him a shower. "Okay. You have ten minutes, then I'm out of here."

He grinned, flashing his famous dimple, and chucked her under the chin. "You're a peach, Ellie."

She swatted his hand away with a glower, her bad mood made worse at her automatic response to that sexy dimple. Something about that indentation made her knees weak. "Don't call me Ellie."

But she was talking to his back as he loped for the stairs. Mmm. He was grace in motion.

Annoyed she'd noticed, she turned her attention to the two-year-old. "Sorry to tell you this, kid, but your dad is a jerk."

"Jerk," Troy echoed, making Elle cringe. Exactly what she needed, for Max, The Beast, to complain to her boss that she was teaching his kid to call him a jerk. Even if he was one.

Thinking of her boss, she moved to the living room and set Troy down next to her on the gray leather couch. A formal room done in classic shades of black, gray and silver, its shining central jewel was the large, mirror-polished black grand piano. For show, no doubt.

"Nice, but I just can't visualize The Beast playing 'Chopsticks.'" Not many sports stars were into classical music. Not in her experience. Which was one reason why she didn't date sports enthusiasts, especially sports stars. To get where they were meant devoting their lives to the sport. She wanted more from life than the next win.

Digging out her phone, she texted Ray Dumond about the events of the night.

Troy slid off the couch and began flipping through a magazine on the table-size ottoman. He crumpled pages and ripped a few here and there, but it kept him occupied and he wasn't screaming so she let him play. He looked up and grinned and she just wanted to pick him up and hug him.

Oh, no. She hardened her heart against the sweetness of his smile. No getting attached to the little beastie. Her time in his life was definitely temporary.

But she did feel for the little guy. She took such joy from her young niece and nephews that it hurt her to think of any child suffering. And neither of Troy's parents were exactly winners in her eyes.

Her phone rang. Her boss. That was quick. She hadn't expected to hear from him for a couple of hours. She answered and filled in the details he asked for. They worked out a strategy for the morning, then disconnected.

She yawned and blinked, really wishing she had time to get in at least an hour's sleep before hitting the office at a run. A glance at her watch showed it had been twenty minutes since Max had trotted off to the shower. That was it. She'd done all she had time for tonight.

"Come on, kid." She swooped up Troy and headed for

the stairs. "I hope Daddy's decent because ready or not, here you come."

On the upper landing she listened for the shower but heard nothing. Turning left she walked down the hall, looking in doors until she found the master suite. And found Max sprawled facedown on a king-size bed.

Just wonderful. Thankfully he'd pulled on a pair of knit boxers, which saved her modesty if not his. The soft fabric clinging to his taut backside did little to disguise his assets.

Her gaze rolled over his long, muscular frame as she carried Troy to the bed. For all his sins, the man had one fine body. The problem was he knew it, and used it. Luckily, she was immune.

She'd never been attracted to Neanderthals.

Okay, that was a lie. Sometimes she just wanted to shimmy up that hard body and sink her teeth into his lower lip.

And then he'd open his mouth and save her from herself. Thank goodness.

Plus she'd learned her lesson where he was concerned.

It killed her that she found him so attractive. Especially as she'd vowed to find a man with more going on in his life than a love of sports.

She knew people thought her a tad unyielding when it came to her stance on men and sports. They didn't understand. Not even her own family understood. She'd had a good childhood, had been, and still was, well loved. But she'd been a girlie girl in a household of athletes.

From the stroller on, she'd been dragged from one brother's sporting event to another, often going to two games in the same day. Sure she enjoyed a good game, but she also wanted to learn how to cook, to paint, to play the drums and go to dance class. She liked to shop and get her nails done. She longed for conversation that didn't include a play-by-play of game highlights.

She'd spent too many years sacrificing her desires to the demand of the majority to easily surrender her future to the overwhelming call of the game.

So, no jocks for her. She wanted, she deserved, a man with varied interests, a man who enjoyed the symphony or the opera, who liked to read and go to the theater, who liked to hike and wasn't afraid of the mall.

Finding one was the problem.

Pulling her gaze from the father, she turned back the covers and tucked the son into the bed as best she could, considering Max was on the outside of the brown comforter.

Troy looked at her with big blue eyes. "Donna?"

Her heart broke a little for the tiny fellow. She smoothed the sheet over his chest.

"Donna and Mama went bye-bye. You're going night-night with Daddy."

"Don't wan' Daddy. Wan' Donna."

Elle didn't blame him. Was there anyone less qualified to raise a child than Max Beasley?

Knowing nothing of the kind, she said, "I'm sure they'll be back soon. If you go to sleep, Mama might even be here when you wake up."

"Night-night?"

"Yes, close your eyes and everything will be better tomorrow." At least she hoped so. The kid deserved better from both his parents.

He nodded and closed his eyes.

Elle bit her lip. Poor little guy. Because she couldn't help herself, she kissed him lightly on the forehead before rising to her feet. She only moved two steps before he popped up.

"You stay," Troy demanded.

"No." She shook her head. "Daddy's here. I have to go home now."

"Daddy seeping." His eyes watered and distress tightened his features. "You stay!"

"It's okay, sweetie," she tried to soothe him, "Daddy's here with you. I have to go to work."

"No. You stay." He threw himself back on the bed and started screaming.

"Fudge sticks." Elle hurried back to the bed. "Troy, stop that now. Daddy's sleeping."

The boy turned his back to her and continued to screech at the top of his lungs. Goodness. She'd heard fire trucks less shrill. Elle waited for Max to wake up, but he slept on, obviously out for the count. Unbelievable.

The kid was turning red. She panicked a little; she couldn't just let him scream himself to sleep.

"Troy, enough. Come here." She lifted him into her arms and rocked him gently. He weighed next to nothing but he was strong. At first he fought her, but after a few minutes he relaxed against her shoulder.

When she thought he was sleeping, she tried to put him back in the bed. He woke and frantically shook his head, clinging to her. Resigned to staying until he slept peacefully, she carried him down the hall and found his nursery. As soon as she stepped inside, he began to scream.

She immediately backed out of the room and the screaming stopped.

"Okay, that's really getting old," she told the boy, her nerves frazzled around the edges. "I'm doing my best here. So no more screaming."

He patted her cheek, and she knew she was being played by a two-year-old. And then he wrapped his little arms around her neck and whispered, "I miss Donna."

His grandmother, not his mother. Any subconscious sympathy for Amber disappeared. Her neglect of her child went way beyond these missing hours and bordered on the criminal.

The faces of her young niece and nephews rolled across her mind's eye. She was such a softy when it came to kids she couldn't just stand by and let Troy suffer.

Okay, all right; Elle stopped fighting her aggravation with the situation and decided to do everything she could to help Troy. If that meant working with Max, she'd do it. But from what she could see, putting Troy in Max's care only moved him from one mostly absent parent to another mostly absent parent.

Troy deserved a happy home with people committed to his emotional and physical welfare.

Which meant Elle had some hard questions for Max. If he couldn't give Troy what he needed, maybe they'd have to redirect their efforts.

Determined to get the kid settled, she made her way to a guest room and lay down with him.

He immediately slipped from the bed and pulled on her hand. "Daddy."

Now he wanted Daddy? Feeling a bit like a yo-yo she allowed him to drag her back to the master suite, where she eyed Max with evil intent. *Wake up and take care of your kid already.*

Digging deep for patience and channeling her new resolve, she tucked Troy back into bed beside his father and sat on the edge of the mattress, prepared to wait until the boy fell asleep.

He smiled at her and pushed the blanket aside. "Night-night."

He wanted her to lie down? With him and The Beast? So not a good idea. But she was exhausted and a glance at the clock on the nightstand told her this was her only chance of getting any more rest before work. She set her cell alarm for forty minutes and stretched out on the very edge of the bed.

Troy scooted close and within minutes his little body went lax in sleep. Elle considered leaving, but couldn't get her eyes to open. The corner of her mouth twitched. The kid had gotten her into bed on their first meeting.

And she was in bed with The Beast. Nobody could ever know. Least of all Max.

It was her last thought before she drifted away.

A kick to the gut woke Max. Instantly alert, he powered up onto his arms and flipped over, ready to fight. A hard lesson learned from his time on the streets.

But it was only Troy turned sideways in the bed and reaching for more territory. That didn't surprise him as the memory of last night flooded in.

Now, seeing the ever-efficient Ms. Austin also sharing his bed, that caused a brow to rise. And other body parts, too.

Long and lush with a waterfall of vibrant red hair, the woman made him want. Too bad she had the personality of a piranha.

Had he imagined her in his bed? Hell yeah. Had almost gotten her there last year at the Gala before he came to his senses. He'd love getting tangled up in those long, pretty legs, but getting entangled in a relationship? That was a no-go. And she had *picket fence* written all over her.

The idea of a street rat like him with Daddy's little princess was ludicrous. The sex might be great but he had nothing more to offer her. Money and fame didn't keep a couple together; he'd seen that often enough in the league. Seriously, what would they talk about?

What the hell? Since when did he worry about conversation with a woman? Never.

Which only served to show he was in a weird place.

He sat up on the side of the bed, scrubbed both hands over his face. And then he looked at Troy. His son.

Max had been on his own forever. The truth was hockey fit him to a T because he didn't play well with others. What he contemplated was insane. No, it was beyond insane.

He was leery of letting a woman into his life. At least he'd know what to do with Elle if he gave in to that insanity. But taking on Troy? He'd barely survived bottles and changing diapers.

But he'd made up his mind. He was going to bring Troy to live with him.

Amber had messed up for the last time.

He glanced at the clock. Saw it was close to six. No doubt Elle would want him to wake her, send her off to work. But the sight of Troy sprawled out sound asleep between them decided him against that course. He wasn't risking waking the kid.

But he did need to make plans for more permanent arrangements. The kid had responded to Elle last night, calming from his screaming jag much more quickly than he ever did for Max. That was recommendation enough for him. Reaching for his phone, he stepped out of the room and made a call to the Director of Public Relations.

Quickly laying out his problem, he asked for Elle's help for the morning.

"I need her here," Ray Dumond stated. "The Jaden issue requires immediate attention. Damn, Max, couldn't you exert a little control?"

"I was under perfect control."

"You know what I mean. The men listen to you."

"Jaden was already buzzing when we got there. He was reminded of the rules. There wasn't much more I could do except guard his back."

"That's something, I guess. No one was seriously hurt?" Dumond showed concern for the first time.

"We take a bigger beating on the ice. Ray, I need Elle for a few hours. And then I need your help. I'm going to claim custody of my son."

"You already have custody of Troy. You made sure of that as soon as you had confirmation he was yours," Ray reminded him. "I've never understood why you pay that witch when you don't have to."

"Because she's his mother. Because I don't know anything about raising a kid. Because I'm always on the road." Because he'd thought she had to be a better bet than he was, but this latest stunt had proved him wrong.

This wasn't the first time she'd left Troy with someone and not bothered to show when she said she would. But it would be the last. He'd warned her what would happen if she left Troy at risk again. Leaving him with a stranger was the last straw.

"He barely knows me, Ray. It's my fault," Max confessed. "I should have tried harder." Amber had caught him in the oldest trap known to man. And he admitted he'd been resentful. Unfortunately Troy was the one to suffer. But that ended now.

"Ray, I need help. It doesn't have to be Elle." In fact, he preferred almost anyone else. "Maybe that new girl, Jenna, can help me. I have the minimal setup for him here, most of which he's outgrown. I need to find a nanny. And it won't take long for the press to get wind of this. You know Amber will make trouble. We need to be prepared."

"You're right about that. It would have been bad if this woman took Troy to the police." Ray's knowledge confirmed Elle had already filled him in on the events of the night before. "Okay, I'll give you someone to help, but you owe me a player event for this, no skipping out on the Gala this year. And I want something from you for the auction. And you were right the first time. Elle is the best one for the job. Let me talk to her."

Max stepped back to view Elle asleep in his bed. How perverse of him to take delight in her presence there. And how appalled she'd be if she were awake for this conversation.

She really was lovely. When she was asleep.

"She's lying down with Troy and we just got him to sleep. Can I have her call you later?"

"Yeah. Listen, I need to know how bad this could get. People expect hockey players to be rough, they'll forgive a little wildness. As long as no innocents are hurt. Tell me straight, Max, what's the worst Amber could say? Any kink, any slaps, we need to know now so we can protect you and the team."

"Ray, what's with you and Elle? Is that what you really think of me?"

"Max." Ray sounded weary now. "I've been around too long not to ask the questions. Be happy I'll believe what you tell me."

"Why does the world care what I do in bed? Why can't I just play hockey?"

"You can, but you won't get eight million dollars for it. Celebrity is a part of the entertainment package you signed on for. Now, do I have anything to worry about?"

Max bit off a curse and spilled his guts. "Kink is relative, isn't it? We had a good time but there were no whips and chains, if that's what you're asking. And I've never hit a woman." He rubbed a knuckle over one thick eyebrow. "But it doesn't really matter what I say, because I don't doubt for a minute she'll lie to get what she wants."

"And she wants Troy?"

"She doesn't care about him or she wouldn't leave him with strangers. She wants the money that comes with him."

"Did you get the name of the girl she left him with last night? We need to get a statement from her before Amber can get to her."

"Elle got it."

"Yes, Elle would. Good. She'll know how to take care of this. Do what she says. What was that noise?"

The sound of Max's teeth grinding together. But beggars couldn't be choosers, so he unclenched his jaw. "Nothing. Anything else?"

"Yes. Be nice. I want Elle still to work for the Thunder organization when she's done helping you."

"Very funny."

"I'm not making fun." Ray barked out the words. "I've seen the friction between you two, and this is too important to muck up. I expect professionalism from both of you." There was a pause. "I've got another call. Send Elle in as soon as you can." The line went dead.

Growling his displeasure with the whole situation, Max returned to the bedroom in time to shut off Elle's alarm before it woke her or the boy. Max eyed the bed. Troy had moved into Max's space and Elle had rolled toward the middle. The only space big enough for him was next to her.

Max could have moved Troy, but where was the fun in that?

Feeling ornery, he climbed in behind Elle's lush form and, pulling her to him, laid his head next to hers on the pillow. Her hair tickled his nose and the sweet scent of cherry blossoms filled his senses. For all of a moment he savored how delicious she felt in his arms before sleep knocked him out.

CHAPTER THREE

ELLE WOKE UP wrapped in the arms of a man. And he was warm and solid and it felt really, really good. And right, they fitted.

Disoriented, she opened her eyes and stared into the blue eyes of a toddler sitting next to her in the bed. She blinked, as much to kick-start her brain as to clear her vision.

And it worked; she remembered the midnight call from the jail and driving Jaden and Max home. Remembered the brunette dropping off a coat that turned out to be Max's son, Troy. And that's where her mind tripped up; this must truly be a dream. Or maybe a nightmare, because no way had she actually climbed into bed with Max Beasley.

Yep, that must be it. A dream. Complete with sensory perception, the baby's tug on her hair, the whisper of the man's breath on her neck, the smell of soap and coffee. And the feel of a warm, hard male along the length of her back.

She closed her eyes and willed herself to wake up, but she couldn't concentrate with the feel of strong arms holding her close. How long had it been since she'd woken in the arms of a lover? Not since she'd broken it off with Brad, which was—well over a year ago.

Too long by far.

"Wake up." A soft hand patted her cheek. "Mama."

Not even close, kid.

Wait. Coffee?

"You know, it's amazing," drawled a sleep-husky voice. "I can actually feel you thinking. What surprises me is you haven't jumped up screaming about your virtue. I knew you really liked me, Ellie."

Elle stiffened at the first sound of his voice and then she scrambled until she sat up against the black leather headboard. She glared down into eyes much more alert than his voice implied.

"I thought I might be dreaming," she declared. He grinned at that. "But I was right the first time. I'm in the middle of a nightmare."

"Now tell the truth, Ellie." His smile never dimmed. "You know you're crushing on me."

Troy crawled up the bed and into Elle's lap. Without thinking about it she kissed his light curls.

"I know you're a sophomoric moron. And my name is Elle." She eyed the coffee cups steaming on the night-stand behind him and debated with herself whether it was worth reaching over him to get to one.

As she couldn't do so without coming into intimate contact with his bare chest, she chose to set Troy next to Max and then scooted to her side of the bed and walked around. It might not be graceful but it was safer.

Avoiding Max's smirking gaze, she caught sight of the time.

"Ten after nine! Shoot, shoot, shoot. How could you let me sleep so long?"

"Calm down. I just got up myself."

"You've been up long enough to make coffee."

"Coffee doesn't count. I'm not awake until after I've had a cup."

Anger roared through Elle. She'd like to argue with him but how could she when she felt the same way? And it was really good coffee, too, which somehow made it worse.

"It's still your fault." She reluctantly set the cup down and began looking for her shoes and socks. "You knew I needed to get into the office early today to do damage control for Jaden and you deliberately took advantage of me last night."

He lifted one dark eyebrow. "I'm pretty sure I didn't take advantage of you last night, or we'd both be in a much better mood this morning."

"This is not funny." She shook a finger at him. "This is my job. You're golden, but I have to earn my spot every day." Spying her shoes under the bed, she went down on her knees to grab them and then bent to see if her socks were under there, too.

"You can stop looking for your shoes and thank me. I called Ray and you're mine for the day."

Elle popped upright and stared at Max. That couldn't be right.

"Excuse me, you did what?"

He propped himself up against the headboard and crossed his arms over his massive, bare chest. "I called Ray and told him I needed your help today. So you're not late."

"I am not going to thank you." To hide her reaction she continued the search for her socks. This was so not good. What must Ray be thinking? No doubt he believed they were sleeping together. She'd probably arrive at the office to find her desk packed and her keycard revoked. Ray had a strict hands-off-the-players rule.

"You said you just woke up yet you've had time to make coffee and call my boss?"

Troy clambered into Max's lap. He flinched and quickly resettled the boy. "Careful of the jewels, kid." To Elle he said, "I talked to Ray earlier when Troy kicked me awake at seven."

"Max, I can't take a full day to babysit for you. We're really busy at the office right now. We have the Jaden issue to deal with, the press is all over us about the rivalry series coming up with the L.A. games and the annual players' Wish upon a Puck benefit for the San Diego Hope Cures Foundation is only three weeks away." She spotted her socks inside her shoes and rolled onto her butt to pull them on. "I don't have time for this."

"This isn't about me." He swung his legs over the side of the bed so his shin rested against her arm. "If I merely needed a babysitter, I have a hundred women I could call who would be happy to help me, and all of them would be a lot more accommodating."

"I bet." She barely kept herself from snorting. "So do me a favor and call one of them."

"Ray said I could have you."

She hoped that wasn't true.

She threw him a give-me-a-break glance and used his knee to leverage herself off the floor. She turned to see Troy playing peek-a-boo with the covers. He stared up at her with guarded blue eyes.

She wanted nothing more than to sweep him up and hug him better. Instead she hardened her heart. She bent to kiss his mop of blond curls. And immediately reminded herself to stop with the kisses. It was hard because she was so used to being free with her affections when it came to kids.

"Be good for Daddy," she told him and then headed for the door. "I'm going now."

"I told you, this isn't about me." Max followed hot on her heels. "It's about Troy. I'm finally going to do what I should have done two years ago. I'm going to bring Troy to live with me. Ray said you'd help me."

Elle stopped and spun around. "Are you serious?"

She didn't know whether to applaud his decision or be worried for Troy's welfare.

"Dead serious." He glanced around to where Troy squirmed around under the covers. "Will you help?"

"A custody battle will be a public nightmare."

"I have custody. But it'll still be a nightmare. Amber won't make this easy. But I have to think of Troy. This isn't the first time she's not returned when she said she would. She's done it to me, to her mother and a few others. But this is the first time she's left him with someone I don't know. I'm not okay with that."

Elle bit her lip and reluctantly nodded. For Troy's sake she'd help Max. She really had no choice if Ray had already committed her.

"I'll talk to Ray. We'll put together a plan. But first I need to go home to shower and change."

"You can do that here," he insisted. "I'm sure I can find something for you to wear."

"No, thank you." She continued on her journey toward freedom. "I'll think better in my own clothes."

"That's the most ridiculous thing I've ever heard."

"I highly doubt that. I've heard some of what's said in the locker room."

His hand wrapped around hers, derailing her escape. And suddenly hard arms surrounded her, pulling her close to all that exposed skin, and his mouth, warm and inviting, settled on hers.

Immediately her arms came up between them and her head went back, breaking the lip-to-lip contact.

"What do you think you're doing?" she demanded.

"Huh." He didn't seem to hear her. His pupils were dilated and his gaze held an odd flare of anticipation, as if he'd found something fascinating. "Kissing you. And I want more."

His head dipped and he claimed her mouth with his as he shifted her so she rested in the crook of his arm. She stiffened, ready to fight, but oh, he felt good. And sleep deprivation must be getting to her because he seduced her by softly deepening the kiss, by rocking her gently against him, by disarming her with pleasure.

With a bold sweep of his tongue he shared his taste as he sipped from her in turn. The man tasted better than coffee and was just as potent. She wanted to melt into him and absorb all his heat, savor the passion he sent rushing through her blood. Which was exactly why she pushed him away again.

"Max! Stop it." She pushed at his shoulders. "Are you insane?"

His sapphire eyes focused on hers. "Apparently, because I liked that a lot. I was hoping to change your mind about leaving."

"Well, you haven't." She tried to step back, but his arms tightened as he stared into her eyes.

"Come on, Elle, we both know the animosity between us is a defense against an inconvenient attraction."

"What I know is we already made this mistake and you found it easy enough to walk away, which means you're only using me now. And my answer is no." She refused to accept that the sizzle between them held any depth. Or that it was mutual. He'd already proven he found her totally resistible.

"Is that what you think?" He lifted hungry eyes from her lips to her eyes. "That was me running from trouble."

"Yeah? Well, nothing has changed. Let go, Max."

This time he released her. She immediately stepped back, but he grabbed her arm, holding her in place. And she saw why when she glanced down and saw Troy standing underfoot.

"Daddy." Troy tugged at Max's sweatpants, and Max swung the toddler into his arms. He appeared unaffected by the embrace, except for the color riding the sharp lines of his cheekbones.

Troy instantly held his arms out to Elle. She shook her head.

"What should I do while you're gone?"

"Change him, feed him." She turned to leave. If he could pretend to be unmoved so could she. "If you're going to be a full-time dad, you'd better get used to it."

Max stepped into her path bringing her face-to-face with father and son, an innocent and a beard-shadowed ruffian. What a mismatched pair, and Max wanted her to bring them together.

"I'm not messing around," Max snapped, snagging her gaze with an intent stare. "I can change a diaper. That wasn't what I was asking. Don't try to blow me off, Elle. If you're not back here in an hour, I'll personally see to it that your next job is ticket-taker. Are we clear?"

"Too clear." She pulled free and hurried down the stairs. When she made the turn at the bend he still stood there watching her. Emotions seething, she stopped. "I know you're used to violence on the ice, but intimidation isn't going to work in this situation. It's going to be about the law and what's best for Troy. It's going to be about appearances and using professionalism and persuasion to get what you want.

"This is my arena," she reminded him, "where I'm the stud. You'll need to do what I say, when I say, how I say. If you have a problem with that, you can take it up with Ray." She waited a beat and when he simply scowled at her, she demanded, "Are we clear?"

His eyes flashed his displeasure, but he gave a sharp nod.

"Good." She offered him a smile that was all teeth. "The first thing you should know is I don't respond well to threats. I'll be back when I've showered and changed."

Pleased to have put him in his place, she hid a real smile and continued down the stairs.

"Pick up some breakfast, will you?" He tossed the directive down at her. "I don't keep food in the house."

She ground her teeth together, aware he'd put her in her place. Miserable man. He needed help all right, but not her. They were oil and vinegar; it would be a mistake to work together. She needed to talk to Ray, to fix this.

As soon as she got on the road, Elle called her boss. She wanted to hear it from him that she was to give her time to Max.

"Elle," he greeted her briskly. "What's the status on Max's situation?"

She gritted her teeth at the clear indication Max had been telling the truth. "I wanted to talk to you before I got too far in my planning. Are you sure the team wants to get involved in Max's private drama?"

"Ordinarily I'd say no, but the press is going to be all over this and I'd prefer to be ahead of the game. A press conference might be too overt," Ray speculated, voicing one of Elle's concerns. "Max is trying to do the right thing by his son. We need to get that out before Amber can make him out to be the bad guy."

"Ray, a bandage isn't going to fix this. It's going to take a full-scale plan to rearrange his life on a personal front and a strategic campaign to change the public's persona of him."

"Exactly. So what's the problem?"

She cleared her throat. "Are you sure I'm the best one for the job? There's the Jaden incident I should be working on."

She couldn't tell him she disliked The Beast, that would be unprofessional—true but unprofessional—and she wasn't going there.

But she didn't want to risk any more close encounters with Max either. She'd melted like wax when he put the lip-lock on her. Just like last time.

Clearly she couldn't trust him. Or herself.

Running from trouble! As if that was an explanation for ditching her—

No, she wasn't going there. The past was better left in the past. To bring it up would infer an interest she didn't have. And couldn't afford.

"There're the new team commercials to finish up this week," she reminded Ray. "Plus I'm working with the printers on the brochure for the owners' meeting at the end of the month."

"So get Jenna to help you." He dismissed her workload. "It's that or I assign her to Max and I'd rather not do that."

Everything in Elle rebelled at that option. Elle had taken the girl under her wing and mentored her. Jenna was fresh and bright and enthusiastic. She had a lot of talent and potential, but she still held the players in awe. The Beast would eat her alive.

Not to mention this deal had disaster written all over it.

Jenna would be out of her depth and Max would walk all over her, which meant Elle would probably be called on to fix anything that went wrong. She chewed on her lower lip, knowing it would be so much better to be in control and prevent those mistakes from happening to begin with.

But if things went south, she could kiss her plans for advancement goodbye. And with Max's kiss still tingling on her tongue she knew she risked everything if she took the job. She made one last stab at salvation.

"Are you sure this situation doesn't require your special touch?" she asked hopefully. After all he was retiring, his career couldn't be hurt.

"No time. I have to hold Natalie's hand for the whole Wish upon a Puck gala event. It's only three weeks away now. The woman can't make a decision to save her life. Tell me again how I got stuck with this assignment?"

"You and the owner go way back and his delicate daughter knows you and feels comfortable working with you, because she knows you're a pushover."

A snort came down the line.

"See, that's why I need you on this Beasley issue. You see the big picture and can cut through the bull. What's it going to be? Are you going to take it on or should I send Jenna over?"

"You know he'll just push her around."

"And she's not your little sister. It's a tough business. The blinders have to come off some time."

Dang it. Dang it. Dang it. Elle sighed. If she didn't take it she'd be letting both herself and him down. And in her heart she knew she'd be letting Troy down. Hadn't she vowed to do her best by him last night?

"I'll do it. But you have to back me up, Ray. Tell him my word is law."

"I already have," he told her as if he'd never been in any doubt she'd agree. "Keep me in the loop. I'll be monitoring the situation. And Elle."

"Yes?"

"This is a sensitive issue and I trust you to be on top of it. I know you have your eye on the directorship when I retire next year. Handle this right and you'll be sitting pretty."

With that the line went dead.

Elle slowly closed her phone. It was already ugly.

Making it through this assignment with her job intact might be the least of her worries. She was going to have to do her best to not outright kill the man.

"If you have custody, why is Troy living with his mother?" Elle thrust a fragrant bag branded with familiar golden arches into Max's arms when he opened the door to her almost exactly an hour later.

"Really?" He popped a hash-brown potato stick into his mouth and pulled a sausage-and-egg sandwich from the bag. "She's his mother, and I travel more than half the year."

"Huh. So why petition for custody to begin with?" She powered through to the kitchen, where he'd set up Troy in a high chair with cereal loops on the tray.

"Because I prefer to be the one to say how much I pay for child support." He unwrapped the sandwich, cut it in half and gave part to Troy.

"What do you pay her?" Elle asked as she sat at the island and pulled a computer pad from her purse.

"Why? What difference does it make?"

She sighed. "This is going to take a really long time if you're going to question everything I ask. I need to get a feel for this situation before I can format a plan."

He considered that, saw the sound reasoning. Still, he hated discussing his private life, exposing vulnerabilities to a near stranger, no matter how good she tasted.

"Four thousand a month. And I bought a house for them in the best school district in San Diego."

He wasn't cheap, damn it. But he didn't like being taken advantage of and Amber had crossed that line when she deliberately got pregnant.

Emptying the fast-food bag, he poked a straw into an orange-juice carton and added it and some hash browns to Troy's meal before taking the rest to a seat on the opposite end of the island from Elle. He looked at the pile of sandwiches and potatoes and grunted in approval. At least she recognized a man his size required a decent amount of food.

He frowned, noticing Elle wore her usual buttoned-up, straight-lines professional wear, with her hair once again pinned up in a tidy bun. He much preferred her in the clingy sweater and swinging ponytail. But now he thought of it, he should be happy for the professional armor she insisted on wearing. It helped to remind both of them that their association was totally work-related.

What had possessed him to kiss her?

He'd wanted her help, of course, and had thought to get his way by the usual means, a little charm, a little unemotional sex. Who knew her frozen facade hid such a wanton?

He did. He could tell himself he'd forgotten her taste, the perfect fit of her in his arms, the way she lit up with passion. But he was lying to himself.

He thought about that for a heartbeat, two. And decided he could live with that.

"Is the title of the house in her name or yours?"

"Mine."

"Does she have a job?"

"No."

Just like at the Gala, one taste of her and he'd known

he needed more, which should have warned him to walk away. Again.

Instead he'd sampled her a second time. A mistake because he already longed for more. He studied her lips even as he remembered Ray's orders to stay clear of her. Max wasn't much for rules but he decided to behave himself. He needed her help.

Plus he valued his freedom. And his family jewels.

Now he thought about it he'd clearly experienced a touch of temporary insanity when he suggested they had a mutual attraction. That was just plain nuts.

"So," she continued her interrogation, "by taking Troy, you're threatening her livelihood?"

"Yes. And she'll fight tooth and nail to keep it."

"Have you had concerns about Amber's care of Troy before now?"

"Not really." He shook his head. "Mostly because she's not the one who usually takes care of him. Her mother does. Donna's great with Troy."

"So what's changed?"

"Donna met a guy who lives in Las Vegas. He's in town two or three times a month for business. And now she's been flying over there to see him. I've got the feeling Troy's the only thing keeping her here, and I expect that to change soon."

Elle typed away on her pad. "So more of Troy's care has fallen onto Amber."

"Yeah. Or, more accurately, onto whoever she can con into taking him. And then she forgets he exists until she's ready to come back again." And the woman had the nerve to call him an absentee father. "It was bad enough when it was me or her best friend she left hanging. I didn't know this gal. I'm not putting up with it anymore."

"That's understandable." She clicked a pen against the

counter, her honey-brown gaze assessing him. "You don't want Amber to be responsible for him anymore. But are you really ready to take on the responsibility yourself?"

"You've already asked me that."

"Yes, but I don't think you've really thought about it. You can't simply hire a nanny and that's the end of it. You will be responsible for his emotional, physical and spiritual welfare. You'll have to put his needs before your own. Are you ready to do that?"

Stuck on *spiritual welfare,* he had no immediate answer.

"Max." When he focused in on her again, he was surprised to find her standing in front of him. "Do you love Troy?"

"He's my son." The answer was automatic.

"I get that, but it doesn't answer my question."

"It's going to have to do." He'd had enough of her intrusive questions.

"Why? Because you don't love him?"

"Do you think his mother does?" he taunted, his exasperation getting the better of him. "Wrong. He's a meal ticket for her. Nothing more. At least I provide for him."

"Yeah. At least."

He pushed to his feet so he towered over her. "What do you want from me? I never wanted a kid. I don't really know how to relate to him. I'm only trying to make sure he's safe."

"By taking him away from the only home he's ever known?"

"By putting him in a safe environment where he's not likely to be dropped off at the nearest police station because the person watching him is tired of waiting for his mother to come collect him." He turned to pace away. "Doesn't sound too loving to me."

"Maybe not, but from what you told me, it sounds like his grandmother does love him. And you aren't exactly known for your ability to commit. He's the innocent here. He deserves tons of love and attention. I'm not convinced you can give it to him. And if I'm not convinced, the public isn't going to be convinced."

"Look, I don't have all the answers right now. But I've made up my mind. Do you want to hear I'll work on the affection part? Fine, I'll plan playdates. The important thing is I can provide for him and keep him safe. So lay out your strategy and let's get started."

"Max." She placed her hand on his arm. "I admire what you're trying to do here, but I don't think you realize the impact it's going to have on your life."

He laughed, and even he heard the bitterness buried in the sound. "Having a kid has already impacted my life."

"Not as much as this will."

Her eyes were earnest, and he realized she really cared about his decision. Not that it was him she was worried about. Her concern was all for Troy.

And why did that tick him off? He neither wanted nor needed her sympathy.

"There is another option, you know," she said softly.

The hair lifted on the back of his neck, giving him a bad feeling about this. "Yeah? What's that?"

"There are a lot of good people out there who could give him the home and love he deserves. You could give him up for adoption."

No. The suggestion shot through him like a bullet through skin and bone, tearing at his composure and resolve, shattering his sense of self. He was independent, a loner, didn't need anyone.

He swung away from her, moving jerkily around to the other side of the island. He needed to get away from her, away from the suggestion he'd tossed at Amber so easily three years ago.

Hands splayed on the granite counter he leaned forward and drilled Elle with a lethal glare. "That's not an option."

Across the way Elle mimicked his pose, totally unintimidated as she leaned forward to challenge him from mere inches away. "Why not?"

Because short stuff was the only family Max had, and that mattered more than he'd counted on.

"Seems I care for the kid more than I realized."

CHAPTER FOUR

SEEING HIS INTERNAL STRUGGLE and the truth of his decision in his navy blue eyes, Elle nodded. She'd had to brace herself to ask the tough questions, but she was glad she had. She felt better about his commitment to Troy.

She sat back and pulled up a spreadsheet on her computer pad.

"This is the plan Ray and I worked out." She swung the pad around so he could see as she read through the plan.

- Determine legal position
- Get Troy a respectable nanny
- Show Max in a good light
- Press

Max's expression went totally blank as he read the list. As she'd expected, he zeroed in on the third item.

"'Show Max in a good light'?" he read out loud. "Explain."

"Simple, really. Everyone expects this to get ugly so it's important to build up your goodwill with the community now to stand you in good stead when the situation heats up."

"And what do you feel is necessary to garner this goodwill?"

"A few public appearances, mostly team events like the blood drive this weekend and the Wish upon a Puck Gala later this month. Maybe we can find a charity you can endorse. That kind of thing. This is where we need your input." She pointed to the press bullet.

"We can either dig into our list and get as much done as possible before the press gets wind of the situation, or we can release a statement so we control the information they get."

"Hell." He flexed his shoulders as if to adjust a heavy weight. "This is all so involved. I simply want to raise my kid. Why does it have to be so complicated?"

"You asked for help. This is us helping." Hand on her hip, she challenged, "What exactly do you object to? Other than the public appearances, of course. We both know how you feel about those." He'd only ever done the minimum his contract called for.

"Isn't that enough?" He gestured angrily at the screen. "Why does it have to be so public?" He shook his head. "I don't like it."

"Do you doubt Amber will make it public?" She kept her tone even, calm in contrast to his ire. "I got the impression you expected her to take her case to the press."

"Hell." He growled his irritation.

"Exactly. Max, we know what we're doing. Is a positive public opinion necessary for you to retain legal custody? No, but your fans want to believe that under that gruff exterior you're a decent guy, one who wouldn't take his child away from his loving mother."

"Loving mothers don't abandon their children."

"The public doesn't know about that. And if you come out and say what a bad mother she is, you look bad for leaving Troy in her care. Yes, you're doing something now, but it takes a lot to sway sympathy away from the mother. You're straddling a fine line here."

He sighed and leaned over the spreadsheet. "So we want control."

"That's my preference, yes. I'd really like to get you and Troy in the public view right away so it's not such a surprise you have a child. And to get the public on your side. How much time do you think we have before Amber surfaces?"

He scowled. "Your guess is as good as mine. Could be ten minutes from now or a week from now. She knows I have Troy, which could send her racing home. Or free her to hang out for another week."

"You haven't heard from her?"

"No. I did hear from Donna. Amber hasn't called her either."

"What did Donna say when you told her you were taking Troy?" Elle wondered, knowing the woman cared deeply for her grandson.

"'It's about time,'" he said, his tone resigned. He wet a paper towel and swiped it over Troy's face. "And then she cried."

"Oh." Elle cringed a little, sympathetic to the woman. "Is she going to be okay?"

"Yeah." Max used the paper towel to sweep the crumbs on the high-chair tray into his hand before tossing the works into the trash. "Now she can accept her beau's proposal with no regrets."

"She's getting married?" At least something good might come of this whole fiasco.

He nodded as he lifted Troy out of the high chair and set him down on the floor. "She said to look for an invitation soon."

"Good for her." Elle entered the info in her computer pad.

"You think so?" Max demanded, his gaze on Troy as he ran toward the family-room sofa.

"Of course," she confirmed, surprised at his reticence. Then she got it. "You were hoping she'd continue to watch Troy."

"He knows her. It would have made the transition easier for him."

She couldn't argue with that. And though she believed his motives were more selfish than he let on, he was thinking about Troy. That was a good thing.

"Don't worry. We'll find a good nanny for you," she assured him and then redirected him to the schedule she'd worked out. "Since we don't know how much time we have, I suggest we get as much done today as possible. I made an appointment for us with Legal at eleven. And I have a contact at the zoo who says a bunch of Scout troops will be visiting tomorrow. I want you to take Troy over there."

"Why?"

"Because it's a great photo op."

"You want me to go to the zoo and hang around until someone asks for a photo? Wow, I'm surprised you trust me to handle it on my own."

She went still and studied him. He stared back looking both impatient and annoyed. Surely he knew he couldn't just loiter around hoping for a photo op. Then she realized he probably didn't.

The man was a phenomenal athlete, a real demon on the ice. None of the players were more disciplined or worked harder. She knew he had a rep for being the first in and last out of the locker room. And he was smart; intelligence snapped in those navy eyes. But he didn't like the limelight, so no, he probably didn't know he simply had to go have fun at the zoo for a couple of hours and the media would find him.

She could see him standing around out front waiting for someone to approach him. Like that would happen with the fierce scowl he wore. True, the frown was as famous as his slap shot, but most people didn't get to experience it up close and personal like his opponents, teammates and the staff did. It could be very off-putting.

"You're right. I'd better come with."

The scowl darkened. "Oh, come on. I'm sure I can handle a bunch of Cub Scouts."

"It's not you I'm worried about."

"I'm not going to hurt a child." He opened the refrigerator for a bottle of water, but she could hear she'd offended him.

"Of course not," she agreed, watching the muscles in his throat work as he drank. "But you're not going to have any fun either. Yes, we have an ulterior motive for going to the zoo. But it should still be fun."

"Fun." He said it as if he had no concept of the meaning of the word.

"Yes. Lighthearted adventure, taking joy in your surroundings, antics and frivolity. Fun."

"I know what fun is." The look he flashed her held none of the elements she'd listed.

"Hum. Knowing what it is and participating in it are two different things."

"Yeah, well, a trip to the zoo to get my photo plastered in the tabloids is not my idea of fun." He tightened the cap on the water bottle with a vicious twist.

"No? Then think of Troy." The boy had found the TV remote and turned on cartoons. "He's at the age to really enjoy the animals." Her nephews certainly loved the world-famous displays. "From the sound of it, you haven't taken him before."

He shrugged dismissively. "Between practice, games and travel I don't have a whole lot of leisure time."

"But you're going to start making time, right? You can think of tomorrow as your first playdate."

"Whatever." He mocked her. "Let's get this show on the road."

"Good idea. I'll dress Troy while you change."

"What's wrong with what we're wearing?" he demanded.

Elle sighed. Was everything going to be a fight?

"You look like you slept in those shorts." He wore a team T-shirt with wrinkled khaki shorts that left half his long, hair-dusted legs bare. A livid bruise on his right shin served as a colorful reminder of his violent occupation. "And Troy did sleep in his."

His lips firmed, causing the scar on his chin to flex, not unattractively. "That's because he's outgrown everything here. Not that there was much. He usually has a bag with him when he visits."

"What about the backpack the gal left?" She looked around trying to remember what she'd done with the bag when she came in last night.

"I checked. There's nothing more than a jacket and some training diapers."

"I'll add shopping to the list." She typed as she spoke. And then she stood. "I'll check out his drawers. Too small may be better than dirty. You need to update his room, too. He wasn't too happy to see the crib last night. And I haven't seen any toys around."

"I'll change." He reached behind him and grabbed a handful of shirt and pulled it off over his head. Elle gulped at the sight of his impressive pecs, the broad stretch of his shoulders. "But, Ellie, try to remember you're helping me with my image. Leave the raising of my son to me."

The morning flew by. And Max thanked his lucky stars for the progress they made. For all her bossy ways, Elle did get things done.

Not only had she set up the appointment with the team's legal department, she'd asked for an attorney specializing in child-custody cases, which resulted in Harold Jones being present at the appointment. Harold had been Max's attorney when he'd originally sought custody.

Because Harold was already aware of the history, it didn't take long to bring him up to speed. And they'd been able to get a plan put together.

Harold would document Amber's actions with Child Protective Services, starting with a statement from Candi. And Max would work on his image and stay away from Amber. When she contacted him, he was to tell her he was exercising his right to take custody of Troy. And then he was not to engage with her in any way.

Fine with him. He couldn't remember whatever it was that drew him to her in the first place. Alcohol had played a large part in it.

Which was why he didn't get drunk anymore, why he hadn't had alcohol in a bar since she'd told him she was pregnant.

Elle sat in on the session with Legal, but at least she'd asked first. He hated sharing his business, but it was easier to let her listen in than to have to recount it all for her afterward. She already knew most of it anyway.

He glanced her way as he drove south on 5. She wasn't entirely bad company when she wasn't squawking orders at him. Except to give him a destination, she didn't try to tell him how to drive and she didn't chat for the purpose of hearing her own voice. Plus she paid attention to Troy, making sure he had what he needed and answering his questions.

Now she had her phone in her hand, which he knew held her schedule. She frowned at the screen and chewed on her sumptuous lower lip, and then she nodded and informed him.

"We have time to get lunch if you want."

He did want. Her lower lip looked yummy.

"Sounds good," he said, turning his attention back to the road. "What do you want to eat?"

"Doesn't matter." She sent him a rueful gaze. "I like it all. Food is one of my weaknesses. There isn't much I don't like. Except oysters. Just yuck."

They were passing Old Town so Max decided Mexican sounded good and pulled off the freeway into the small lot of a restaurant famous for its homemade tortillas.

"Good choice." She applauded his selection as she opened the back door to release Troy from his seat. Another item that needed to be replaced. He wondered where shopping ranked on that schedule of hers. Not that he looked forward to the excursion. Maybe he could talk her into doing it for him.

No doubt she considered shopping fun.

After they got settled at the table and ordered their food, Max sat back and sipped his tea.

"Okay, we talked to the lawyers. We interviewed employment agencies and we have appointments to meet prospective nannies on Sunday. We got the statement from Candi the lawyers wanted. What else is on your agenda today? Remember I have to be at the sports arena by five o'clock."

"Of course." She placed a chip on Troy's high chair. "You have a game tonight. The nanny agency confirmed a sitter. I sent the info to your cell. I think we've done all we can for today. But I've started a shopping list for you if you want to venture out later."

He tossed her his most charming smile. "I was hoping you might take on that chore for me."

She shook her finger at him. "Dream on. I have plans tonight."

"Oh yeah, what?" What kind of man yanked her chain? Probably an accountant or a banker, the responsible type who rode a desk and got his exercise at the gym.

He leaned forward, resting his elbows on the scarred wooden table. "You know, some women actually like me."

The corner of her mouth twitched before she pressed her lips together. "They don't know you like I do."

"No," he lifted his focus from her lush mouth to meet her gaze, "*you* don't know me like *they* do." He saw the memory of their kiss bloom in her eyes, in the rush of pink to her cheeks.

Oh yeah, she remembered. And he hadn't forgotten. Everything about her screamed hands off, except the taste of her and the feel of her in his arms, both of which he recalled all too well.

"If they knew you the way I know you, they wouldn't know you the way they do."

He laughed. "You don't even know what you just said."

"I do," she assured him. "And you do, too."

"So tell me, what do you know about me that the other women don't? What makes me so terrible?"

"I don't think this conversation is a good idea." She offered Troy a sip from his cup of water.

"Why not? Do you think you'll hurt my feelings?" He shrugged off the notion. "Don't worry. I'm The Beast. I can take it."

"Exactly." She crossed her arms on the table, the posture plumping her bust up so a nice hint of cleavage came into view in the V of her white blouse. "You're a beast. You're selfish, bad-tempered and arrogant. Your puck bunnies see a bad-boy athlete, a celebrity. I see a jerk."

"Jerk," Troy echoed and laughed.

"Hey." Max tugged on the boy's earlobe. "That's Daddy to you."

"Jerk Daddy."

Max's gaze shifted to Elle. "Thanks for that."

She shrugged. "I told you we shouldn't have this conversation. Or is it that you really can't take the truth?"

"Ellie, Ellie, we both know if it weren't for the rules, you'd have a whole different opinion."

She lifted one dark-russet eyebrow. "If it helps your ego to blame the rules, you go right ahead."

"I get the feeling you're big on rules."

"I like order, and rules help keep order. So yeah, I'm big on rules." She wasn't defensive, simply stating a fact. "Your whole career revolves around rules. I'd think you'd understand." Then she rolled her eyes. "What am I saying? I forgot I was talking to the team's biggest rule-breaker."

"If you want to win, you have to be willing to go to the boards every time."

"A sentiment the team appreciates."

"Oh, no. Don't do that. Don't get political on me now."

"Fool. Ah, lunch."

A visual feast filled the table as the spicy aroma of grilling meat and vegetables sizzling on a hot skillet tantalized his appetite. Max rubbed his hands together, ready to dig in.

The sound of Elle's laughter caught his attention. He looked up to find the waiter flirting with her over her fish tacos. A hard-eyed glare sent the man on his way.

They may not be involved but the waiter didn't know

that, and Max would be damned if he'd let another man chat up his woman right in front of him. And with the taste of her still in his head he was perverse enough not to want to see another man paying her attention.

"I don't know why you call me selfish." He placed a plate with a small amount of rice and refried beans on Troy's tray and handed the boy a spoon. "I'm a generous guy."

"You're not stingy or cheap." She licked a smudge of guacamole from her finger, making Max's mind fog for a moment. "That's not the same thing."

"It's mostly the same."

She cocked her head and considered him. "No. Tell me, besides spending time in the penalty box, the last time you did something you didn't want to do."

He frowned. Jaden's birthday party came to mind. But no, he liked spending time with his teammates on occasion. The whole bar scene was what was getting old. He enjoyed a good barbecue or pickup game of football or hoops more these days.

"Nobody likes doing things they don't want to do."

"True. But they do them anyway, either out of duty because it's expected of them, or because someone they care about wants them to. You don't put yourself out for anyone."

"No? Then why have I been jumping through hoops all day?"

She inclined her head. "I guess you have me there." She glanced at Troy, who was covered in rice and beans. Max grimaced and reached for a napkin as she taunted with a touch of glee. "And today's just the beginning."

"Stop, Daddy." Troy fought Max's efforts to clean him up. "No."

"I'll admit I'm going to need help." He played humble. "So how about it, Ellie, will you help me out with the shopping?"

"You don't fool me." She narrowed her brown eyes at him. "And call me Ellie one more time and you'll be on your own."

He grinned for real, flashing his dimple. "We both know you won't desert me. You're too ambitious and Ray is retiring next year. I suspect you have your eye on advancement."

"Maybe. But I have my limits, so don't push me."

"We worked well together today." Surprisingly. "You were helpful with Candi. She didn't want to give a statement against Amber, and she was suspicious of me and Harold."

The attorney had insisted on accompanying them to get the statement. He wanted fresh details and to hear the information for himself. His participation would hold weight when he passed the statement on to his friend at Child Protective Services who would get the statement on record.

"It helped to have another woman there," she agreed. "But you're the one who made her see Troy was the one suffering for Amber's behavior. You were gentle, charming and sincere. That's what made the difference."

"I have my moments. So it's agreed, you'll help me out." He made it a statement.

"Right," she scoffed. "I take care of all your pesky little jobs and what do you do for me?"

Acknowledging she was no dummy, he inclined his head. "You do a good job on this and I'll put in a good word for you with the powers that be."

She shook her head, light flowing from the nearby window flickering like flame in her dark red tresses. "My work will stand on its own merits, thank you very much, especially if it gets as ugly as everyone keeps saying it will. No," she chided him, her smile both challenging and a little smug, "you can do better than that."

He leaned back in his chair. As a competitor he did enjoy her pep. Bossy with a touch of feistiness.

"What did you have in mind? A bonus? That can be arranged."

"I don't want your money, Max. I want your cooperation."

Okay, that raised the hair on the back of his neck. The woman was in the process of rearranging his whole life. What more could she want from him?

"Chip! Chip!" Troy demanded loudly and hit his tray to add emphasis to his need.

After a glance at Max, Elle responded with a quiet request for the toddler to lower his voice and ask nicely.

He got louder and made a grab for the chip basket.

"Troy," Max said in warning.

"Chip, Daddy." Troy began to cry.

He didn't relent. "Stop that crying now. What did I tell you?"

He pointedly moved the chips out of Troy's reach. He didn't reward bad behavior.

But Troy saw him move the chips away and began to shriek at the top of his lungs. Every head in the restaurant turned in their direction.

Only years of controlling his emotions kept Max from cringing. He gritted his teeth instead. From past experience he knew he'd lost the upper hand; any attempt at discipline now would only make the scene worse. But Elle hadn't learned yet and she turned censuring eyes on him.

"Aren't you going to do anything?" she challenged.

He was about to take the boy outside but decided to see

what she'd do. He shook his head. "He'll stop in a minute."
Well, he hoped. Sometimes the jags went on for a while.

"If you don't handle it, I will."

Max waved his hand, inviting her to try. If she had a magic trick to stop these fits, he wanted to know about it.

She leaned close to Troy and spoke quietly to him. The boy shook his head and shrieked louder. Elle didn't hesitate; she stood up and lifted Troy from the high chair and then the two disappeared outside, Troy's wails fading in their wake.

Ten minutes later she walked in with a subdued Troy. She tucked him back in his chair and then slid into her seat.

"Do you want a chip?" she asked him.

"'Ess pease." The boy nodded.

She placed a couple of chips on his tray and gave him a pretty smile. "Good boy."

Her brown eyes flicked up to Max's, encouraging him to acknowledge the good behavior. Hoping for a smile of his own—maybe that was her magic—he ruffled Troy's hair.

"That's my good boy."

Troy grinned at him around a bite of chip. "Jerk Daddy."

Max glanced at Elle, and yeah, there it was: a smile of approval. Something in his chest tightened. The silent praise and joint sense of accomplishment warmed him in some odd way.

Yep, powerful magic.

To hide his reaction he lifted a brow at her, challenging her over the moniker his son had given him. Her smile blossomed into a grin.

She lifted a shoulder and let it drop in a one-sided shrug. "It's a work in progress."

CHAPTER FIVE

"So TELL ME, ELLIE," Max drawled as they stood in line at the stroller kiosk at the zoo, "is this really your idea of fun?"

"Not this part, no." She let the "Ellie" slide this time. She'd decided the more she protested, the more he'd use the nickname to torment her. "A stroller is on your shopping list."

When he simply shrugged she nudged his arm with her shoulder. "Quit being a spoilsport. It's seventy-five degrees on a sunny afternoon in December. You're going to be strolling around the world's greatest zoo. Give it a chance."

"I've never been around animals much," he said dismissively.

"No pets as a kid?" she asked before she remembered he'd grown up in foster care.

"None that belonged to me."

That was telling. "And you never wanted a dog?"

"As a kid it was easier not to want what you couldn't have."

"Of course. A stroller, please," she told the teenage girl behind the counter. Max tossed down his credit card. "And now you have custody of Troy. In a few years you can get him a dog."

"Maybe. Someday. It doesn't really make sense with all the traveling I do." He took control of the stroller the teenager indicated.

"Excuse me," the young blonde addressed Max, her eyes starstruck, "we're not supposed to ask, but can I have your autograph?"

"Sure." Max winked at the girl and scrawled his name across a brochure. "I won't tell."

She cradled the pamphlet. "Thank you."

"Okay, that was a good start." Elle applauded his inter-action with the teen. "You've been recognized."

"Great. Which way to the Scouts?"

She rolled her eyes. "It doesn't work that way. Now we wander around, check out the animals and have fun. My nephews love this place. I've been thinking of get-ting an annual pass."

Max just shoved his hands into his shorts pockets.

"Well, Troy and I will have fun. Look, he's excited to be here."

The two-year-old sat forward in the stroller and pointed at the monkeys in the enclosure. His eyes lit with joy, he pointed and yammered excitedly. His words were totally incoherent, but his animation spoke volumes.

"Yeah, he is." Max crouched down next to Troy. "Hey, short stuff, that's a capuchin monkey. Cute, huh?"

"Monkey." Troy giggled when one of the creatures came right down to the front of the enclosure and sat in the corner. Troy waved and the monkey's paw went up. Then the animal gave a shriek and scurried and swung himself up to a tree limb next to his buddies, high up in the enclosed space.

Max, Elle and Troy weaved their way through the mon-key exhibits. Halfway along Max lifted Troy out of the stroller and let him run free, the two bonding as they laughed over the animals' antics.

The boy just drank in his father's attention. It was good to see them having fun together.

They were both so needy. Her heart broke for them, especially for Troy. But she couldn't, wouldn't, let her emotions engage. Once she helped Max get a plan set, her role in Troy's life ended. If she let him get attached to her, he'd only suffer again when she disappeared from his life.

For both their sakes, she needed to maintain her detachment.

"Okay, this is cool," Max conceded as they moved on to the gorillas.

"Yeah, it is. How did the two of you do last night? What do you think of the sitter the agency sent over? Do you think she might work out long-term?"

"Not in the slightest. It was a total disaster. I had to rush home from practice because he had a screaming fit." He met her gaze, an unlikely plea in the back of his blue eyes. "Would you watch him during tonight's game? He's been through a lot the last couple of days. We'd both feel a lot better if he was with someone familiar."

She really should say no; spending more time with these two was a bad idea. But the thought of a distraught Troy screaming for hours twisted her gut into knots. *Softy,* she chided herself as she nodded.

"Elle, you are a peach." He gave her ponytail a tug and then turned back to the trail.

He'd called her Elle. Ah, progress. She smiled and tagged along with the mismatched pair.

Occasionally she joined in the fun and laughter but mostly she let them have this time together. Watching them play she felt better about them as a team.

The Scouts found them near the pandas and Max graciously signed everything thrust at him, yet he made a point of making Troy a part of the process.

She'd already texted her friend in the zoo's PR department and nodded when he waved to indicate he'd gotten all the pictures he needed. People were getting pictures from all over and she snapped a few, too, for the team. Mission accomplished.

"Where to next?" Max asked when the latest group of Scouts scampered off.

"It's three-thirty. We need to head out if you're going to make it to the arena on time."

"But we haven't seen the lions, the tigers or the bears."

"Pandas are bears."

"Doesn't count. They're cuddly."

She laughed and turned the stroller in the direction of the exit. "You had a good time."

"I did," he readily agreed, his reluctance to leave evident in the longing glance he sent toward the sign indicating the bears were in the opposite direction. "You were right about this place."

"You'll have to come back when you have more time."

"I will." He pulled a cap out of Troy's backpack and put it on, instantly becoming less recognizable. "Troy had a ball. He even liked the Scouts, so it wasn't so bad doing the autograph thing. The kids really seemed to get a kick out of it."

"Are you kidding? You made their day. Most PR events are lighthearted and fun, even when we're helping to promote something more serious. I don't understand why you're so averse to participating."

"Because I feel like a fraud."

"A fraud," she repeated, mystified by his comment. "I don't understand."

"I'm just a guy who plays hockey. I don't know what all the hoopla is about."

"How about the fact you have some of the most impressive stats in the NHL." She never would have guessed he held this streak of modesty. His ego and confidence levels were off the charts and well earned; the stats didn't lie.

"Yeah, but the whole celebrity thing isn't my gig." He took over pushing the stroller as they started up a short incline. "I'm no more special than the person asking for the autograph."

"To them you are. You represent the American dream, the best of the best. Half of them want to be you, the other half want to date you."

"You just made it worse."

She eyed his profile suspiciously. It was his lack of expression that tipped her off. "You don't fool me. You know all this."

The corner of his mouth rolled up in a half grin and he inclined his head. "Doesn't change how I feel."

She hooked her arm through his, ignored the damage his dimple did to her knees and sent him a sideways glance. "You need more practice. And I'm just the girl to help you with that."

Troy fell asleep on the walk out of the zoo but Max still took the time to stop and buy annual passes.

Elle used the opportunity to check her messages. She was only through the sixth one when he joined her.

"You know, don't bother taking us home," she said. She'd met him at his place for their trip to the zoo. "I've decided to go with you to the arena. We have an office there and I can get some work done while he's sleeping."

"Okay," he agreed as he strapped Troy into his seat. "But he probably won't nap for long."

"I'll take what time I can get."

At the arena Max carried Troy as Elle led the way into the empty director's office on the press level. Jenna would be in the outer office covering the game later so Elle could focus on getting some work done while Troy slept.

She moved ahead of Max into the room and pushed together two armchairs to make a bed for the sleeping boy. Max carefully laid him down. Troy stirred, blinked and then turned over and sank back into sleep.

"All that running around at the zoo wore him out." She carefully placed her sweater over him. "I expected him to wake up on the trip in."

"Yeah, he sleeps like the dead."

"Yuck." She wrinkled her nose in disgust.

Max shook his head in obvious disdain at the sensitivity of girls. "He also kicks," he warned. "So don't be startled if you hear movement."

"That's good to know. Thanks." She held out her hand palm up. Before she could ask for his keys, he cupped her hand and brought it to his mouth, pressing a warm kiss in her palm. Her knees went a little weak, as tingles of awareness sizzled along her nerves.

She found herself leaning toward him before she snapped to attention, snatching her hand from his grasp.

"What are you doing?"

"Saying thank you."

"Well, don't. This is my job." She reinforced her professional stance by stepping behind the desk, mentally willing her heartbeat back to normal. She really needed to get a grip on her libido. He was off-limits on so many levels. So he had a little humility. So what? He was still a jock, still professional suicide, still a beast.

"I was asking for your keys. Which reminds me. We

never finished our conversation of tit for tat. You know, what you would do for me if I helped you out?"

"Sure we did," he asserted, taking a few steps toward the door. "I cooperate and you handle a few of the more mundane tasks for me."

"Right, let me be clear what I mean by cooperation. First, I do have other assignments, so I need you to be respectful of my time. Don't blow me off, and don't be late."

"Nice—" Sarcasm dripped from the word.

She held up her hand to stop him. "I'm not done. Second, don't ad lib. You've asked for our help, use it. If someone puts you on the spot, say you're running late and ask them to call the PR office to set up an interview."

"I can do that." A little less jerky.

"Good. Third, do not engage with Amber over anything. The lawyers said it and I'm repeating it. After you've told her you're keeping Troy, let us and the attorneys handle her. She's going to try to draw you out. Don't let her."

He stood, hands on hips, contemplating her. His expression was blank as his eyes ran over her. She braced, ready for an icy set down.

"That's a lot of cooperation," he said, his tone deceptively mild. "What am I getting in exchange?"

"You said shopping." Easy enough for her to do but something men despised, at least her brothers always had.

"I'm going to need more." He reclaimed the distance he'd given up so he loomed in front of the desk.

"I don't think so. I already gave you the last two days."

He shook his head. "That's the job. You already made that clear."

She sat down and immediately regretted the decision to do so. The man towered over her. She spread her hands on the desk.

"Do you want my help or not?" she demanded as if the sheer size of him didn't intimidate. As if her skin didn't still tingle from the feel of his mouth against her palm. "You're due on the ice in twenty minutes."

Eyes narrowed on hers, he reached into his pocket and set his keys on the desk.

"And your credit card," she demanded.

He braced both hands on the desk and leaned forward until their noses nearly touched. The predatory gleam in his navy gaze sent the blood rushing through her veins.

"This conversation is not over."

She lifted her chin. Met him stare for stare.

"I have four brothers," she informed him. "Threats don't work with me."

He straightened, reached into his pocket for his wallet and tossed down a black card. And then he leaned over until his breath heated the sensitive skin behind her ear.

"I'm not your brother," he warned, the threat in his voice sending a shiver down her spine.

Without another word he turned and strode from the room.

Max palmed his phone after leaving Elle's office and hit the number for the private investigator recommended by Ray.

He'd lost that round. But he wasn't as upset as he should be. The woman stood her ground better than some defensemen he knew. He had to respect that.

The investigator picked up and Max asked for a report.

"She's in Phoenix. She hooked up with one of the Coyotes during your last home stand. Jones Anton. They partied pretty hard here and she followed him home, moved the party to Phoenix. They've been hitting the clubs nightly."

"Is she staying with him?" Max demanded though he knew the answer. She was a clinger and players were her thing.

"Yeah." The confirmation came down the line. "It's not the first time. I talked to one of his teammates. He said Amber and Jones have been connecting whenever Phoenix played San Diego for the past four months. The Coyotes are at home for another five days. Do you want me to make contact? Let her know she's needed at home?"

"No," Max instructed. "Just keep tabs on her. Let me know when she's headed home." Elle wanted time, Max would give her time. The longer Amber was away without making contact the worse it would look for her. And he needed every advantage he could get.

Elle had really slayed him when she'd suggested putting Troy up for adoption. Max realized some of the resentment he'd been harboring against Amber had rolled over to Troy. But the thought of giving him up gave Max a new perspective, revealing raw emotions he'd never experienced before.

He had no illusions about himself. He knew he was emotionally stunted. Raising Troy was going to be the ride of a lifetime. But Max was in it for the long haul.

"Beasley. In my office now," Coach called as Max strode across the locker room.

He changed his course, propped himself in the doorway. "Yeah?"

"Have a seat." A stocky man in his fifties, Coach pointed to the visitor's chair. "You're late."

Max made a point of looking at his watch. "We have fifteen minutes before we need to be on the ice. I'll make it." He turned away.

"Sit down. You're late for you. You're usually here an hour early."

Max sat. "I have some things going on in my life."

"So Ray told me." Coach clasped thick fingers together on the desk. "You want to talk about it?"

"No." Living it was exhausting enough.

Coach nodded and light bounced off his bald dome. "Let me know if that changes."

"Sure." Max made to rise but Coach stopped him with a raised hand.

"I'm not done. Ian isn't going to be back for eight weeks. I'm going to be assigning an interim captain while he's on the injured list. You're my strongest man on the ice. I want you to take it on."

Max started shaking his head before Coach finished. "I'm not a leader. You know that."

"I know you think that, but the players respect you. They listen to you. You're leading without even knowing it."

"Ask Tank. He's solid, has maturity."

"Tank is a great goalie because he's very reactive. Proactive? A strategist? Not so much."

"Coach…" Max sighed.

"I want you to think about it. And think hard. The team needs you." Coach picked up a pen, tapped it against the blotter. It wasn't like him to vacillate. "The exposure could help your image."

"So this is coming from Ray?" Max carefully kept the anger out of his voice. So that was it. He was grateful for the PR department's assistance, but he'd be damned if he'd let them interfere with his play on the ice.

"Hell no. I'm the head coach." Totally intent, Coach leaned forward in his chair. "I don't take coaching instructions from anyone. You're disciplined, aggressive on the ice and always looking to improve your skills. You'd be a dream player if you weren't such a damn loner."

"I have to get on the ice."

"You want to win, don't you? You work harder than anyone. The next eight weeks takes us through the middle of the season. To have any hope of reaching the play-offs, we need to come out of it with a winning record. We've taken four losses since Ian was injured."

"One of our starters is out. We just need to regroup."

"Horse puckey." Both hands hit the desk as Coach surged to his feet. "We need a leader on the ice. You're always three moves ahead. The whole team needs to get to that point. You can get them there. You have a natural talent and it's time to capitalize on it for the team."

"I want to win."

"Good." Coach beamed and rubbed his hands together. "I'll make the announcement at practice."

"Hold on." Max stopped him. "I want the cup as much as anyone, but I've got a lot going on right now. I have to make time for my kid."

Coach's face fell. "I have a family. I respect where you're coming from. But the team needs you. It wouldn't be much different than what you're doing now except for sitting in on the coaches' meetings. You already give me a weekly report on the team's performance. You'd just have to share the information with the players."

Max pushed to his feet. Just to get out of there, he gave Coach the answer he was looking for. "I'll think about it."

"Elle!" The name carried clearly on the brisk night air to where Elle stood waiting with Troy outside the superstore in Point Loma.

She smiled even as she turned, warmed by the familiar sound of her friend's voice. Michelle had called while Elle was buckling Troy into his slightly-too-small car seat. Elle had offered to wave off her shopping trip to meet up with her friend who was only in town for the night, but Michelle suggested she join Elle instead.

Michelle looked lovely as usual in a waist-length leather jacket and jeans tucked into black high-heeled boots. Her long blond hair flowed softly past her shoulders.

"You look fabulous." Elle hugged her longtime friend. For a moment she flashed back fifteen years to Princess Camp where she'd met Michelle and Amanda, or Sleeping Beauty and Rapunzel to Elle's Belle from *Beauty and the Beast.* Those summers had been life-changing for her. "Love obviously agrees with you."

"I'm happy." She simply beamed. "Life has never been better."

"I'm glad," Elle said, and she was, but Michelle's happiness just served to showcase the shambles Elle's life was in at the moment. She craved order and for the next few weeks she was responsible for a man whose entire life was in a state of chaos. She loved Michelle, but yeah, Elle was a little jealous.

Putting her petty feelings aside, she introduced Michelle to Troy.

"Well, you're a cutie." Michelle playfully shook Troy's hand before meeting Elle's gaze. "And he belongs to Max Beasley? Hard to imagine The Beast with a kid."

"Exactly. Right? But it's all too real. And it's my job to shop for a wardrobe and outfit a nursery."

"Lucky for you I've just been through this very thing." Michelle hooked her arm through Elle's and turned her toward the store's entrance. "This is going to be fun. Let's go spend The Beast's money."

"How are Gabe and Jack?" Elle asked about Michelle's new fiancé and his ward.

"They're great. I miss them so much when I travel.

Are you sure you can't make it to the club tonight? I can get you passes."

"I'd love to go hear someone sing your songs." Elle remembered the thrill of hearing that Michelle had sold her first song to a rising Nashville singer two months ago. "Any other time I would, but I'd probably fall asleep at the table." She recounted the events of the past two days. "I'm exhausted."

"You slept with Max Beasley?"

Elle rolled her eyes. Of course that's what her friend focused on. "*Slept* being the operative word in that sentence."

"And it took you twenty minutes to tell me? I always knew you liked Amanda better than me."

"Don't pout." Elle gave a fussy Troy her keys to play with. "I haven't had a chance to talk to Amanda either. And you're making this into something it's not." Something it could never be. And no, that was not a pinch of regret.

She stopped next to a rack of baby clothes. "Oh my gosh, look at these tiny jeans. Aren't they the cutest thing?"

"Check out these overalls." Michelle held up a khaki outfit and Elle relaxed, having successfully changed the subject. But her calm shattered a moment later.

"Don't think you're going to get off that easy. The Beast oozes sex. You can't tell me you slept with him and just shrug it off. I know you think the guy is a tool, but he has one fine body." She gave Elle a cheeky grin. "Is he boxers or briefs?"

"Knock it off." Elle rolled her eyes. "Nothing happened. Troy was between us mo—" She cut herself off, but too late.

"Most of the time," Michelle finished for Elle, coming

around the cart and lowering her voice. "Which means not the whole time. Spill."

Elle hesitated, chewing her bottom lip as she retrieved her keys from the back of the cart where Troy had dropped them. To distract the boy from their conversation, she handed him a miniature toy truck from an endcap display. Then she caved.

"So okay, I woke up in his arms."

"I knew it," Michelle crowed.

"Yes, and the man is so hot he almost set the sheets on fire." Elle fanned herself playfully though in truth the memory of those first disorienting moments when she'd snuggled back into Max's arms really did send heat spreading through her body. "But he's still a tool."

"Goes without saying," Michelle agreed loyally. "And doesn't that make for a challenge? We all know how you like a challenge."

"What?" Elle looked up from the toddler jacket she'd pulled from the rack.

"Come on, Elle. Thou protesteth too much. The man has made it into every conversation we've had in the past couple of months. That says something."

"Maybe that I'm venting?"

"I think it's more than that. You're attracted to him."

"Well, yeah. I like chocolate cake for breakfast, too, but I don't give in to the lure of that either."

"Would it be so bad to let him close?" Michelle's tone took on a serious note. "Your love life has been a little slim lately."

"Try nonexistent." Rather than meet her friend's gaze Elle examined the car seats that caught her attention. "But Max isn't the cure. He really is annoying, and sports are his life. Literally. You know how I feel about that."

"Right. No sportsmen for you. You know, you're really

cutting out a large portion of the male population with that edict," Michelle said as if delivering hard news. "And when you cut out married men and same-sex partners, there's not a whole lot left. I thought you gave up on that rule when you tried that online dating service and only got three potential matches."

Elle cringed at the memory. That had *so* not been a good idea. "I've broadened my criteria since then."

"I hope so. I swear one of them looked like a serial killer."

Elle flushed. "They weren't that bad."

"Please. The serial killer was the only one with anything going for him. The other two were clearly mama's boys. Just because Max plays hockey for a living doesn't mean he doesn't have other interests."

"Not that I've seen." Although there was that spectacular grand piano in his living room. Coming from foster care it wouldn't be something passed down through the family. Maybe it came with the house. "Plus I'd rather date the serial killer."

"Liar. The man is intelligent, hot and rich. That's a magic combo for any woman."

"He's also—" She started to say "an arrogant jerk," but looking into Troy's sleepy gaze she bit back the familiar refrain.

It didn't feel quite so valid after encountering Max's unexpected modesty this afternoon. And then there were the groceries. There was no food in his house yesterday so she'd decided to go by his place before coming here tonight to make a shopping list. But the cupboards were full, the refrigerator stocked. Plus the laundry had been done and put away. She'd been blown away.

"He's off-limits," she reminded Michelle. "I'm not allowed to fraternize with the players, remember."

"Stupid rule, if you ask me. A lot of people meet their mates through work."

"It hasn't been a problem yet. I can't believe you're pushing me toward Max," she said, feeling foolish she'd never told Michelle or Amanda about her experience with Max at last year's Gala. "You usually view a relationship for what you can get out of it. Max's life is a complicated mess right now. I'd be a fool to get involved."

"That was before I fell for Gabe and Jack." Michelle's playfulness dropped away, leaving raw emotion. "This love gig is the best thing in the world and I want it for you and Amanda."

Warmth flooded Elle's heart and she pulled Michelle into a huge hug. "I'm so happy for you. Nobody deserves to find happiness more than you."

"I never expected it." Michelle wiped tears from under her eyes. "Being the world's biggest romance cynic. But Gabe wouldn't give up on me, and I'm so thankful he didn't. We've set the date. Late April. You have to be there."

"I wouldn't miss it," Elle promised. Her cell buzzed. She pulled it from her pocket. "A text from Max. He's done with his practice."

For some reason the announcement brought the gleam back to Michelle's green gaze. "Don't be so quick to dismiss your attraction to Max Beasley. Promise me you'll be open to love."

"Enough already," Elle declared with affectionate frustration. "What's your thing with me and Max?"

"Don't you get it? You're Beauty, he's The Beast. It's like it was meant to be."

CHAPTER SIX

Max was late. They were supposed to be interviewing nannies and he should have been here thirty minutes ago.

There went concession number one. Not that Elle was surprised.

Disappointed was another thing. The emotion niggled insistently though she tried to push it away. She'd honestly thought they'd come to an understanding. At least he'd sounded sincere when he thanked her for all her assistance over the past couple of days after she helped him lug in her purchases last night.

She'd already given the ladies an application to complete, but that delay wouldn't last much longer. The slowest of the three had finished a couple of minutes ago.

Elle sighed. She'd wait another ten minutes and then start the interviews without him.

He breezed in halfway through the second interview making no excuses for his tardiness.

Troy looked nice in a new outfit. When he saw Elle, he wiggled in Max's arms, demanding to be put down. Max complied and Troy trotted right to Elle, clambering up into her lap. Affection tugged her heartstrings. She returned Troy's hug with a smile. How quickly the adorable tyke had stolen into her heart.

When he threw his arms around her neck and squeezed,

her insides melted. It took a moment for her to regain her composure.

She noticed he hadn't asked for his mother. Well, not around Elle anyway.

"This is Troy—and Max Beasley." She made the introductions.

"Mr. Beasley." The applicant perked up at the sight of Max, her gaze surreptitiously sweeping over him like a kid looking at a lollipop. "It's so nice to meet you. I'm a big fan."

"It's always nice to meet a fan." He chatted on, charming the woman as he drew information from her.

Too bad. The woman had shown promise. Elle liked her demeanor, pleasant and open, unlike candidate number one.

Still Elle lined through her name on the list. Someone crushing on Max was not a good candidate. He'd be hard enough to work for without adding a personal element to the equation.

From the look he sent her Max agreed.

"Thanks for coming in." Elle stood. "We'll let the agency know our decision." She wrapped up the interview.

"So what did I miss?" He sprawled in the visitor's chair, totally at ease.

Elle handed him the applications. "The second candidate is the one that just left. I spoke to the first candidate before you arrived." Yes, there was censure in her voice. "I asked her to stay in case you wanted to interview her yourself, but in my opinion she's a bit…stiff for an energetic two-year-old."

"Sorry to be late." He offered a belated apology. "Harold wanted me to stop by and sign some papers."

"You could have called."

He cocked a brow at her. "I'll remember that next time."

"Please do."

"So is that them?" Max casually turned to check out the two women sitting in the reception area. Candidate one was tall and thin, all sharp lines and angles from her posture to her wedge-cut gray hair. There was nothing restful about the woman. Candidate three sat next to her, a petite brunette with golden skin and exotic eyes. Slim and pretty, she was the youngest of the three.

"Yes. Should I have candidate one step back in?"

"No. I agree with your assessment. *Stiff* is being kind. And I think Troy could take the small one."

Elle laughed. Then was appalled by the unprofessional response. His answering grin, the intimate moment of shared humor, only made the breach worse. Biting her lips together to hold in a smile, she fought for composure.

"She's probably stronger than she looks." She defended the applicant but even as she said the words she knew it was a no go.

"She'd have to be," he muttered. Then he said louder, "Plus I couldn't trust the guys around her."

"Do you have players over to your place a lot?" She set Troy down and handed him a ball from her bottom drawer.

"Baseball," he announced.

"That's right." She applauded his knowledge. "Don't throw it."

"Not a lot." Max shifted in his seat. "I have a weekly poker game when we're in town and occasionally host other events. Somebody is bound to hit on her, then leave her hanging, and then she'll quit and I'll have to start this process all over again. I say save the time and trouble."

"You're the boss." She gave in because she agreed with his assessment. "Excuse me while I let them go."

When she returned to her desk she gathered the applications together and tapped them into a neat pile. "I'll contact the agency and set up more interviews. I know you're in a hurry to find someone. Can you come back before the game tonight? I have a family event at two but I can probably be here by four."

"That won't be necessary. I have someone in mind for the job." The ball rolled close to Max's feet and he picked it up and rolled it back to Troy.

"Who?" Elle asked, suspicious. Setting up a lover as his nanny would defeat the purpose of any good publicity they managed to gain him. "We chose this agency because of its prestigious reputation in San Diego. We agreed it would help foster your image as a caring father."

"No, you made that decree and I went along with it, but now I've thought of someone else I want to have the job."

Seeing he was going to be stubborn about this, she turned to her computer. "Okay, give me her information. I'll set up an appointment for an interview."

He rose to his feet. "How about we just go see her instead?"

"Now?" She hated the squeak in her voice. "I planned to work this morning."

"It won't take more than an hour. You probably had that much time scheduled for the rest of the interviews."

He was right but she had the bad feeling that once she left the office she wouldn't make it back. On the other hand, he did need a nanny and if she didn't go with him, he might hire the gal without Elle's input. She needed to go along for damage control.

"Okay, but I better not miss my nephew's birthday party. I had a work event last year and had to miss it. Walter was not a happy camper. In fact, I better take my car."

He nixed that. "Troy is better when you're along. I

had to stop twice this morning because he kept trying to climb out of his seat."

That made sense so she grabbed her purse and reluctantly followed him to his SUV. He strapped Troy in and they hit the road headed east.

After twenty minutes on Highway 94 she asked, "Where does this gal live?"

"Jamul."

"Jamul." Good gracious. Jamul was a small burg in rural San Diego where most of the properties were big, far-spread and housed livestock. Was Max looking to make a ranch hand Troy's nanny? She hoped he knew what he was doing. Just because a person knew how to feed a kid didn't mean they knew how to feed a child.

She flashed him a look full of her displeasure. "That's an hour just in driving time."

"We won't be there long." He ignored her ire. "I'm sure she'll be happy for the opportunity."

Elle crossed her arms and settled back in the corner of her seat. "So tell me about this gal. What's her name? How do you know her?"

"Deb Potter. I don't like to talk about my past."

"Really?" she exclaimed, overdoing the surprise. "I'd never know that by all the phone calls I get from the press about how open you are in interviews."

He scowled at the sarcasm. "It's nobody's business."

"No. And the team doesn't require you reveal anything you don't want to. But you have to know, Max, the more you hold back the more they hound you."

"What I do on the ice is all that matters."

"You aren't that naive." Though there were times she wished it were that simple, too. "There's the sport and there's the celebrity, and they go hand in hand."

"I don't have to like it," he groused.

"No. But you're smart enough to use it. I've seen you use The Beast to divert attention away from your personal life."

The corner of his mouth lifted in a half smirk, and he raised one shoulder and let it drop. "They're easily distracted."

"So, tell me about Deb."

His massive chest lifted and then he blew out a harsh breath. "You're like a Chihuahua after a bone."

She cocked her head, decided she could live with that and prodded, "So give me what I want and I'll stop. I'll share," she offered.

He huffed. "What's to know? It's obvious you were the princess of your own little kingdom."

"Oh, I could tell you tales."

He rolled his eyes, then slanted a wolfish glance her way. "You'll like Deb. She kept me in line when I was a kid."

"That's quite a recommendation." She checked the backseat to see how Troy was doing. His eyes were heavy and he was blinking to stay awake.

"You have no idea," Max drawled. "Deb and Pat Potter were my foster parents my last year in the system. They were decent."

Foster care. She sympathized, knowing it could be rough for kids in the system, but she couldn't really relate. She might despair of living among athletes, but her parents were a solid couple, her family tight. Sure her brothers were a pain, but she loved them all.

She didn't know what it meant to be alone. She had her own place but it wasn't the same. Her family were so much a part of who she was that even when she was alone she knew they were there, knew she had their support, knew she was loved.

The way Max protected his past she bet a classification of *decent* said a lot.

"How long were you in the system?" she asked. Sensing he'd detest any sign of sympathy, she aimed for matter-of-fact.

And still silence met her query.

But you didn't survive in a family her size without cultivating a little stubbornness. She waited him out. Most people found silence awkward. Ordinarily, she doubted Max was one of them. Still, it worked.

"I don't remember ever not being in foster care as a child. Ever not feeling like an obligation to someone. Until Deb and Pat."

"Sounds rough."

"Says the princess with the picture-perfect childhood."

"Hey," she chided him. "I admit I had a good childhood, but it wasn't all sunshine and tiaras."

"Come on," he jeered. "I've seen you in the seats with your family, rocking it and having a good time."

"Yes, we're close. But I can also tell you living with four brothers is its own form of hell."

"I was born in jail."

"Oh my God." The shock of it rocked her. And then the sadness of it made her hurt for him. Okay, he won the worst-childhood battle.

His head swung around at her exclamation and his gaze swept over her face but there was no telling his thoughts.

"Sorry," she said. "I can't imagine what it must feel like knowing that."

Eyes back on the road, he shrugged. "You put it behind you. If you don't, it'll drag you down."

"Yes. That I can imagine." Just as she imagined it hadn't been easy. Was this where his unexpected modesty came from? Was it a sense of unworthiness left over from his humble beginnings?

"Your history came up every time you moved into a new home. My mother was a drunk and a druggie. Child Protective Services took me from her and put me in foster care when I was three and she was arrested for prostitution."

"You were an innocent, but you carried her sins with you." Barely aware of whispering the thought aloud, Elle knew she'd hit a sore spot when Max went still beside her.

"A long way from the castle and your princess upbringing."

She let that go because...well, just because. "What about your father?"

Silence, and then a sigh. "I don't know. My birth certificate lists unknown."

And it went from sad to sadder.

"How's Troy doing?" he tossed at her.

She looked over her shoulder. Troy slept in a patch of warm sunshine, his innocence radiating off him like a beacon. She imagined him at the mercy of a mother more interested in her next fix than his next meal and everything in her rebelled.

"That's why you went for custody of Troy," she blurted. "You weren't going to let happen to him what happened to you."

A ruddiness darkened his cheeks and his eyes remained fixed on the road ahead. His very reticence confirmed her insight.

"Good for you." She didn't know why he was embarrassed. She was usually the first one to give him a bad time, but he deserved huge kudos for stepping up for Troy. With his background it would have been so easy for him to turn his back and walk away.

"Don't patronize me," he snarled.

"I'm not," she assured him sincerely. "I admire your commitment to raise him. I questioned your dedication in the beginning, but I understand now why you feel you have to do this."

"You don't understand shit."

Hurt by his harsh rejection, she crossed her arms over her chest and glared out the window. "I understand you're such a jerk you have a problem accepting a simple compliment. In one way you're right. I have no idea what your life was like. I was lucky. I had both parents and doting older brothers. But that doesn't mean I don't possess the sensibilities to understand how a father would want to give his son a better life than he had."

She felt the weight of his stare, but no words came.

She'd been nice to him, and he'd thrown it in her face. The man was a rude brute. *Beast* fit him to a T.

He didn't want to talk? Fine. She reached for her phone and punched up her messages. She had work to do anyway.

Elle and Deb hit it off like a man and his remote control. Sprawled in a narrow wingback chair in Deb's small living room, Max shifted his attention from woman to woman, one stunning with a dark mahogany ponytail, the other a comfortable woman in her late forties with a brown bob.

They couldn't be more different, yet they'd instantly become fast friends.

Troy sat on Deb's lap eating a cookie while the women talked over his head. Yammering like long-lost friends, the women had rippled through more topics in twenty minutes than he did during a three-hour poker game.

"Max, this boy of yours is precious." Deb ran her fingers through Troy's fine blond hair, her expression slightly wistful. "He's grown so much since the last time I saw him. I can't believe it's taken you this long to bring him by again."

"With all the traveling I do, I've only had him for a day or two here and there."

"I understand." She sent him a fond smile. "I'm happy you find time to attend the occasional performance with this old woman."

"Old, my ass," he scoffed at her claim. "You can run circles around women half your age. Which doesn't mean you should be handling this place on your own. Are you ready to give it up yet?"

She shrugged. "The market is soft. Plus where else would I go?"

He jumped on the opening. "That's why I'm here actually. I'm bringing Troy to live with me. I need you to come take care of us."

"What?" Caught off guard, Deb gave a nervous laugh. "Don't tease," she warned. "I've fallen for this little guy and if you're not careful you'll find me lodged in your guest room."

"It's agreed, then." He carefully kept his gaze trained away from Elle. "Pack your bags."

He'd made a fool of himself on the ride out here. Hurt her. An apology wouldn't be out of line. But forget it. He'd told her he didn't talk about his past. She should have respected his wishes instead of delving into his psyche and hitting too close to home.

"I think I'll stay here, thank you." Deb waved him off, obviously not taking him seriously. "But you can bring this little guy out to see me anytime."

"I'm not joking, Deb. You were the best foster mom I had and I need a nanny to help me with Troy. Because of all the traveling I do it should be someone who can live in. I'd be honored if you'd take the job."

"Oh. Oh, goodness." Deb glanced from him to Elle and back again. "You're serious."

"Very serious."

"Max, I can't." Regret shadowed her green eyes. "What would I do with this place? It's been in my mother's family for generations. It was hard enough deciding to put it up for sale. I can't abandon it."

Damn. He'd hoped her Realtor would have contacted her by now. On the way to Elle's office this morning he'd called his accountant and instructed him to buy Deb's property for the asking price plus ten percent. He was to make the purchase through Max's foundation and keep the buyer's name out of it until closing.

Of course his accountant had had a fit, demanding to know what Max wanted with a run-down ranch house and two acres of depleted vegetable plot. Plus he could sure as hell negotiate a better price. Max repeated his instructions and hung up.

He had no definitive idea of what he wanted to do with the property. The vague notion of a sports camp for kids played at the back of his mind. It didn't matter. What he did with the ranch was unimportant.

He wanted to free up Deb.

First, because he didn't like the idea of her living in the back of beyond all by herself. And the acreage was too much for a lone woman to handle. Second, he needed her available to accept his offer to watch Troy.

Max knew Deb, trusted her. He'd be comfortable leaving Troy in her care. But he couldn't let her know he was the buyer. Her pride would get in the way of doing the right thing.

"We'll rent it out. Or find a manager. I need you, Deb.

Amber has left him with strangers. I don't want to do that. I need to know he's in good hands."

"Max," she said helplessly, clearly tempted but torn between duty and longing.

A ring sounded from the other room. Her phone. A faint frown drew her pale eyebrows together, but she excused herself and handed Troy off to Elle to go answer the summons.

"With any luck that will be her Realtor," he muttered.

Elle pinned him with a stare. "That would be coincidental, wouldn't it? Or do you know something we don't?"

"I'm sure I know plenty you don't."

She set Troy on his feet. "You know what I mean."

"I'm sure I don't."

"I'm sure you do." She leaned forward, her expression fierce as she went to battle for her new friend. "She's a nice lady. Tell me you haven't done anything that will hurt her."

"Give me a break." Tired of her lack of faith in him, he got in her face, going nose to nose with her. "You just met her. She's the closest thing to a mother I've ever known. I'd never hurt her."

True to form she didn't back down, but after a moment she nodded. "I believe you."

Deb hurried back into the room, coming to a quick stop when she spied them so close together. Hopeful speculation entered her eyes as she cleared her throat.

"Am I interrupting something? I can give you another minute."

"No," Elle denied too quickly, jerking back into her seat.

Interesting reaction, Max mused, unsure if he should be flattered or insulted.

"Good." Deb eagerly resumed her spot on the couch. "If you really want me to come take care of Troy, I'd love to. That was my Realtor. I have a buyer for this place."

CHAPTER SEVEN

"WELL, THAT WAS worth the trip." Max buckled into his seat. "I'll drop you back at your office."

"No," Elle corrected him. "I'm already late. You have to take me to my nephew's birthday party. Head for Bonita."

"You can go after I drop you off." He pulled onto the road and headed west. "Then you'll have your car."

"You said we'd be an hour," she reminded him. "And we were three. The party started an hour ago. I'm not going to miss this party."

Once he'd got Deb's agreement to help with Troy, Max had pushed for her to start immediately, but Deb had protested she needed time to pack up the house and prepare the property for an extended absence.

Used to getting his way, Max overrode her objections by insisting on helping her to do what needed being done now while Elle arranged for a moving company to pack and store Deb's belongings.

Deb accepted their help, but when it came to leaving, she'd quietly and stubbornly held her ground, insisting she needed a week to take care of things she didn't trust to the moving company.

Elle liked the older woman. She especially liked that she held her own against Max's perseverance. Elle hoped it meant Deb would stand up for Troy when necessary.

"It won't hurt to be a few minutes late." Max tried to argue.

"I'm already more than a few minutes late. It'll be over if I have to go all the way to Point Loma and back. Bonita is on the way."

"Okay, I'll stop and let you out."

"Oh, no." His grudging capitulation irked Elle into messing with him. "I want you to come in and meet my family. Say hello to my nephew."

"I'd rather not."

"And I'd rather you did. I've done a lot for you the last few days. You can do this for me."

"Troy—"

"There's cake. Troy will have a great time."

"What kind of cake?"

Gracious, Elle racked her memory for the information, found it. "Marble with buttercream icing."

"Hmm." He considered the information before nodding. "I guess I can give you half an hour."

So he had a sweet tooth. Good to know.

She needed to find all the good possible in this situation because as soon as she walked through the door with Max her family would make all kinds of erroneous assumptions. She hadn't brought a guy home to meet them since the ninth grade. An event she still had nightmares about.

But it couldn't be helped; seeing disappointment in Walter's big brown eyes tore her apart. She refused to let it happen again.

Max would just have to deal.

Should she tell him? Give him a little warning he was about to be pinned to the grill and slow-roasted for the next thirty minutes? Nah. Not until he met Walter, who was a big fan of The Beast.

It might be mean, but she owed Max a little mean. The

memory of him curled around her in bed solidified her resolve. And Elle knew her sister-in-law had ordered a jumper, so Troy would have a ball.

Twenty minutes later she led the way to the backyard of her brother's two-story subdivision home. The yard was huge, with a pool, patio and lawn, though most of the grass was covered by the large red-and-yellow monster-truck jumper.

"Elle, you made it." Her mother swooped in and gave her a big hug.

"My girls." Dad enveloped them in his arms while they were still wrapped together. The scent of his familiar aftershave and the barbecue tickled her nose as a kiss landed on her head. She reached for him, too, giving her parents an extra squeeze.

"I love you guys," she told them as she often did. Her family believed in hugs and open declarations of love. So what if her voice was a little extra husky and tears burned in the backs of her eyes. Hearing Max's story today had reminded her how lucky she was, and it was all because of these two people.

"Hey, brat," a deep male voice called out, "you going to introduce us to your date?"

Breaking away from her folks, Elle caught the hopeful glance Mom shared with Dad before she turned to address her oldest brother's challenge. She forced a smile when she saw Max's presence had garnered a crowd. Oh, boy.

She pinned Adam with a glare as she stepped over to where Max stood just inside the gate holding Troy in his arms.

"We all know this is the last place I'd bring a date. You all probably recognize Max Beasley from San Diego Thunder. He's here to wish Walter a happy birthday. And this is his son, Troy."

A husky, blond-haired ten-year-old pushed his way to the front of the pack. Walter gazed up at Max with huge brown eyes. "The Beast," he whispered in awe. "You came to see me?"

"You must be Walter." Max offered his huge hand to the starstruck boy. "Happy birthday." His large paw swallowed Walter's small mitt. "I hear you have cake at this shindig."

"Yeah, and it's got buttercream icing, not that whipped-cream junk." Walter pulled Max forward. "I'll get you a piece."

Max threw Elle a you-owe-me look over his shoulder and allowed himself to be dragged away, a passel of kids following in his wake.

"So you're still holding that dinner against us?" Adam murmured next to her ear. "That was twelve years ago. Get over it already."

"Trauma sticks with a person. Hey, Steph." Elle hugged her sister-in-law Stephanie. "I hope you two don't mind that I brought a guest."

"Of course not," Stephanie assured her. "Anytime." Her gaze roamed over the broad-shouldered, slim-hipped hockey player and she hummed her approval. "Especially major-league hockey players."

"Hey. Standing right here," Elle's brother protested.

"I know, dear." Stephanie continued to face Max and the crowd around the cake, but winked at Elle. "Can you get the candy for the piñata while I talk to Elle?"

"Sure, I'll get the candy, but I want me some sugar first." Adam turned all he-man and, grabbing Stephanie, he bent her over his arm in a grand gesture and stole a kiss. Stephanie looped her arms around his neck and the embrace shifted from playful to real in the space of a heartbeat.

Elle left them to it. Obviously passion still existed in the eleven-year marriage and for a minute she envied what her brother had: a beautiful home, a loving partner, kids. Her goals didn't include any of that.

Sure, she wanted love and a family, but it was something that lurked in the future, not something she worked toward, or even encouraged, at this point in her life. It wasn't even on her five-year radar.

The hopeful look in her mom's eyes haunted her. So maybe she'd accept the next time a nice guy asked her out. After all, you didn't find Prince Charming without dating a few frogs.

"Girlfriend, you've been holding out on me." Stephanie hooked her arm through Elle's. "The Beast? Yum. So give, what's the answer to the question on the mind of every woman in San Diego?"

Elle shook her head at her sister-in-law's craziness. "What question is that?"

"Oh, please, you may be focused on your career, but you're not dead. And you are here with him. So is he or is he not an animal in bed?"

"Steph!" Heat flooded Elle's cheeks while she quickly looked around to see if anyone had heard the outrageous question. "I don't know."

"Liar. Those red cheeks tell another tale. We're tight. You can tell me anything."

"Honestly, there's nothing to tell." But the words lacked conviction. She'd been in his bed. And the memory of him sprawled half-naked, all negligent arrogance, wouldn't leave her head.

And she did know what it felt like to be swept away by him, to be held in a heated embrace, kissed until passion ignited her senses. But she tamped those memories down before they could escape. No good would come from re-living that moment.

"Well, then." Stephanie heaved an exaggerated sigh. "Shame on you. He is one fine man."

"He's also a pro hockey player. You know I don't do sports enthusiasts."

"Yeah, I still hope you'll come to your senses about that irrational decree."

"My entire childhood was spent at one sporting event or another. Is it wrong to want more in a relationship than to sit in the bleachers or in front of the TV watching the next game?"

"It's not wrong. But it might well be hopeless. Because, sweetie, all the best men are into sports in one form or another."

Elle met Stephanie's sympathetic scrutiny. "So you think it's too much to hope for a man who enjoys both football and the symphony?"

Stephanie squeezed her arm. "Never give up on hope."

For some reason the comment sent Elle's gaze searching for Max. She found him surrounded by her four brothers by the barbecue. Uh-oh.

"Excuse me." Picking up her pace, she rushed over to save him from the horde.

"I believe your sister just made it clear this was not a date." Max spoke in even tones even though he appeared to be outnumbered four to one. "So if I've kissed her, if I've had my hands on her, it is none of your business."

"Now, that sounds a little suspicious, doesn't it, Brad? Like Max here has indeed had his hands on Elle but doesn't want to claim the appropriate relationship?" Adam leaned forward aggressively. "Did we mention Brad was a cop? You don't have any tickets, do you, Max?" Then his fierce smile turned a little sinister. "And Mike is with the IRS."

"I can't believe you're doing it again." Elle pushed into the male circle to step in front of Max and glower at her towering brothers. "At least in ninth grade you had the decency to take the guy on one-on-one. Now that we're adults, how much more mature to go four-on-one."

"Elle, have you seen the size of this guy?"

"Really," she demanded of Mike, "that's your response? Max is my colleague and you're treating him like a thug. Suppose I called your boss and told him you were threatening people with spontaneous audits. Do you think he'd find it so funny?"

"Nobody said anything about an audit," Mike stated emphatically even as he paled a little.

"That's what I heard. How about you, Max?"

"Leave me out of this."

"See, you've embarrassed my guest." A disgusted snort sounded behind her. She ignored it. She smirked, knowing just how to get back at her brothers for their interference in her love life. "I should tell Mom."

"There's no need to bring Mom into this." Adam took a step back, his gaze shooting around the yard in search of their mother, making sure she was nowhere near to be drawn into the conversation.

"Lighten up, Elle," Quinn advised. "We were just making sure Max understands you have a strong support system. It's for your own good."

She saw red. Nothing infuriated her more than having her right to make her own decisions taken from her.

"Of course, that makes it all okay. So the next time you bring a date home I should ask her about her biological clock. Or maybe I should have asked Stephanie if she made enough as a sales associate at Sullivans Jewels to support Adam? Or better yet I should go ask her to step out front so I can inform her it's not cool to ogle the hockey player."

"Okay, dynamo, that's enough." Max wrapped an arm around her waist, lifted her off her feet and carried her away. "Let's go see how Troy is doing in the jumper."

"Let me down." She wiggled against him but soon stopped. Rubbing her body along the hard length of his in full view of her family and friends seemed a bit brazen. "I'm not going to let them get away with treating you that way."

"You mean, treating you that way." He taunted her. "I'm so lucky you were there to save me from the wolves."

"No need to be snide," she huffed, trying to work her arms between them. "And you're going to want to put me down before I kick you somewhere it hurts. A lot."

"Ah, ah, don't make me find your mother." He let her slide down his side as he set her on her feet next to the jumper.

She bit back a smile. Oh, he was quick. Tugging on the hem of her shirt, she straightened her clothes, pretending she didn't still feel the heat of Max's body burned into hers.

To distract herself she focused on spotting Troy among the rowdy kids. Found him right in the middle of the action, jumping away, having a great time.

"You're an emotional lot, aren't you?" Max observed. "From hugs and kisses to knock-down, drag-out arguments."

She shrugged, a little self-conscious. "All siblings argue. The emotion comes from my mom's side of the family. We're big huggers, every time we see each other and every time we say goodbye."

He grunted, focused his eyes on Troy jumping away. "I hate goodbyes. They're false and unnecessary."

After hearing about his childhood, she wasn't surprised. Saddened for him, but not surprised. Her family must be overwhelming for him. Sympathy softened her mood.

She slowly nodded. "I can see how you might feel that way. How did you handle it?"

"Easy. I don't do them."

"Never?" The pink in her cheeks must have told him where her thoughts went.

"No." He smirked. "Satisfaction doesn't require a goodbye."

"Bragging is a sign of overcompensating."

"It's not bragging if it's true."

"Daddy! Daddy! Look at me!" Troy waved from the middle of the jumper, lost his balance and tumbled to his butt. He lay on his back giggling before rolling over and scrambling to his feet to start the process all over again.

She met Max's eyes and they grinned at each other. He winked and butterflies fluttered in her stomach.

"So you liked Deb?"

The question was so carefully casual Elle knew it was anything but nonchalant. Deb was obviously important to him in ways he didn't even admit to himself. This arrangement wasn't just to benefit Troy but to help Deb. And it was clear to Elle if he hadn't gone in person to ask for her help, Deb wouldn't have left the property.

"Yes. She'll be good with Troy."

Max curled his fingers around the rubber corner of the huge jumper and leaned close. "He'll be good for her, too. I don't know why I didn't think of it sooner. I've hated to see her on her own so far from town."

"She looks like she can handle herself," Elle assured him softly.

"Just because she can doesn't mean she should have to. She deserves better."

"She won't cramp your style?"

"Troy beat her to that."

She rolled her eyes. "You are incorrigible."

"Just telling it like it is."

He clearly believed his decree yet he still planned to make the sacrifice. She had to respect his determination.

Enough of the fan fest already.

"Listen, I understand if you want to leave," she said. "I really appreciate you coming in with me. You made Walter's party a big hit."

"No problem. He's a neat kid." He propped his hands on his hips. "I promised I'd stop by his hockey practice next week. And it's not the worst time I've ever had, even counting the showdown with the fearless foursome. You know you could have given me a little warning."

"Where would be the fun in that?" she shot back. Then sighed because the threat of her mother had been tossed around and the truth was she'd be horrified by Elle's behavior. "I'm sorry."

He yanked on her ponytail, running his hand down the length in a near caress then tugging at the end. The back of her knees tingled.

"Forget it. That was nothing compared to what I deal with daily. Besides, they were just protecting their little sister."

"Well, your half hour is up so it's okay if you want to leave." And why did the prospect of that suddenly seem like a letdown?

The man was more than annoying. Already he'd broken rule number one, wasting her time by being late and then by dragging her out to meet Deb. If he'd worked with her, she could have accomplished twice as much in half the time.

"Nah. Your dad just put a steak on the grill for me. Troy is having fun. I can hang out and give you a ride back to your car."

"What about your game tonight?"

He shrugged. "I don't have to be there until five. We have time. Since Deb can't start until next week, can you watch Troy tonight? I'll figure out something for the rest of the week tomorrow."

"Sure— Ah!" She jumped, startled by her brother Adam's sudden appearance. He took her arm and drew her a few feet away then swung her around.

"I didn't appreciate the way you talked about Stephanie—"

"You're going to want to let her go." Suddenly Max appeared next to her and Adam, his shoulders relaxed, his expression pleasant as he took a sip of soda.

Adam dropped his hand. "This doesn't concern you. It's between me and my sister."

"You're right." Max shrugged. "I just have two words to offer, *time* and *place*."

"Max is right." Elle tried to defuse the tension. "I shouldn't have brought Stephanie into our argument, but you guys drive me nuts with—"

"Elle." Max cut her off.

"What? Oh, right." She focused on Adam. "Sorry."

"We're only trying to look out for you." Adam defended the brothers' interrogation of Max.

"Adam, stop." Stephanie appeared at her husband's side, wrapping her arm around his. "Elle, he only gets this way when his women are threatened. Say you're sorry, dear."

"She's my sister. It's my duty to—"

Unimpressed, Stephanie went onto her toes, cupped Adam's rigid jaw in her hands and kissed him boldly.

Elle glanced away and caught Max staring at her, his gaze as hot as the embrace taking place next to them.

"Don't." To her horror the demand sounded more like a plea.

The smolder intensified. "It's your brother's fault."

Snort. "That's the first time I've heard that excuse."

Stephanie broke off the kiss and pulled back. "Come on, hero. I need help with the piñata." She snagged Adam's hand and led him away.

"Neat trick," Max muttered.

Adam suddenly stopped and swung around. "Elle, I'm sorry. But I can't promise it won't happen again, little sis." His gaze shifted to Max. "You can stay."

Max lifted his chin in acknowledgment. "Okay," he told Elle, "maybe your brother isn't a complete ass after all."

"Yeah." Elle watched the couple's retreat. "And Stephanie is my new hero." She made the mistake of looking back at Max.

She longed for him.

Her heartbeat tripped as fast as the flittering wings of the hummingbird buzzing by. In the middle of a kid's birthday party she nearly squirmed with the heat flowing through her body. And she had the nerve to lecture her brother on the inappropriateness of his behavior?

Right. At least Stephanie's kiss had served to distract Adam from his irrational protective streak. Max actually surprised Elle. As a professional hockey player, aggression was a daily deal for him, yet he'd been the one with the level head. The one to defuse the situation before it could get out of hand.

Which only served to make her want him more. What made it worse was knowing he wanted her, too.

Maybe leaving with him wasn't such a good idea.

She knew better than to believe in the illusion of his interest. All she had to do was remember back to the Gala last year.

For a woman who'd dreamed of being a princess as a little girl the night had been a winter fantasy come true. She'd felt beautiful in her fancy gown and upswept hair. The setting had been magical, a true tropical wonderland at an oceanside resort celebrating the Christmas holiday in sparkling, candlelit grandeur.

Still new to the job, she'd been enchanted to be rubbing shoulders with the players, VIPs and celebrities. Yes, she worked the first half of the evening, but then she was free to enjoy the festivities until Ray needed her help with the auction.

Having broken up with Brad the month before, she'd been determined to have a good time. She'd danced and laughed and flirted, having a great time. She'd been standing in a doorway opening onto the terrace when a couple of the single players stopped, pointed at the mistletoe decorating the threshold and demanded a kiss. She'd obliged them with a buss on the cheek and then waved them away.

She had turned to step out for air and Max stood there. Suddenly she was under the mistletoe being kissed by The Beast. She'd never forget the magic of that moment.

This was no obligatory peck. Instead he cupped her cheek, lowered his head and claimed her mouth in a hot slide of passion that led from one kiss to the next as he drew her onto the terrace into the darkness. Into temptation. Into an erotic interlude out of time.

For the next hour they danced, swaying to the music floating on the air, soft as the breeze drifting off the ocean. He was so strong, moving her with confidence and surety, dipping her over his arm and lifting her into another kiss. He seduced her with equal parts gentleness and demand.

And then it was over. Duty drew her into the room to assist Ray with the auction. As she worked she was appalled at her actions. Ray had made it clear the players were off-limits. And she believed in following the rules.

But her body still tingled from Max's touch and when the auction wrapped up, she looked for him, secretly hoping to be swept off her feet. She found him—leaving with another woman.

Betrayal burned a hole in her stomach as she watched him escort the other woman from the room with a hand on her back. It was obvious they were together, obvious he'd been playing with Elle.

All her secret hopes, all the promise of the evening, all the potential of something special, followed him from the room. She went from flushed and happy to deflated and hurt in the blink of an eye.

The magic of the night turned to dust in a moment.

So no, she wouldn't be leaving with him after all. The less time she spent in his company the better.

CHAPTER EIGHT

HER PARENTS WERE HAPPY to give Elle a ride to her office to pick up her car.

"It was nice of you to bring Max to the party." Her mom glanced back at Elle from the front seat. "Walter was thrilled."

"I thought it was against team policy for you to date the players," her dad grumbled.

"We're not dating— Mom." Elle pleaded for intervention. The men in her life would wrap her in cotton candy and set her on a shelf if she let them.

"Leave her alone, Jim. Elle is entitled to her privacy. If she wants to break the rules with a hunky hockey player, that's her business."

"Mom!"

"Becca, don't encourage her." Dad growled his displeasure.

"Hush," Mom scolded him. "I will encourage her. She works too hard and deserves to find someone special."

Go Mom.

"Thanks, Mom." Elle flipped through her emails on her phone. Maybe she'd get a chance to answer a few before the game.

But she spoke too soon.

Because Mom turned her eagle eye on Elle.

"You can protest all you like, Elle, but it was obvious to everyone at the party that there's strong chemistry between you two."

"You're wrong." Elle did protest because it was her only defense against an unwanted truth. "That was just residual falloff from Adam and Stephanie."

"It wasn't Adam defending you." Becca flipped down the mirror to check her makeup and fluff up her hair. Pride for her beautiful mother burned in Elle. She admired and respected her so much.

Both redheads, with the same slim, athletic build, they'd been mistaken for sisters more than a few times. But Becca's blue eyes and softer features gave her a beauty Elle—with the brown eyes and defined cheekbones inherited from her father, who had a touch of Native American in him—lacked.

Becca met Elle's gaze in the mirror. "It's the way he was looking at you that had your brothers' and father's hackles bristling."

"Okay. There may have been a moment of awareness," she confessed, never able to keep things from her mother for long. "But it doesn't matter, so don't get your hopes up. Dad is right, the team has rules." And so did she. "Max is off-limits. Besides, the truth is I'm a glorified babysitter."

"Is there a problem with his son?" A total mom, Becca immediately latched on to any baby concerns. "Troy seemed like such a sweet boy."

"He is, except for the screaming jags." Elle recounted her experiences with the toddler. "It's a bad habit that's worked for him."

"How did you get him to stop?" Becca wanted to know.

"I held him wrapped up in my arms, told him I wanted him to take deep breaths, and we breathed together. After a couple of minutes, I hummed to him until he settled down. Then I told him I would not put up with screaming."

"And that worked?"

"He hasn't screamed with me again. I don't know about Max."

"He needs a nanny," her dad threw in.

"He hired a nice woman," Elle confided. "She used to be a foster mother of his, but she has to wrap up some things with the sale of her property and can't start until next week. And he's so sensitive about whom he leaves Troy with that I'll probably end up watching him this week."

"I don't know how much help it will be, but I can watch him during the day," Becca volunteered. "Just for a week, right?"

"Yes. Mom, that would be awesome." Elle leaned forward in her enthusiasm. "Are you sure you wouldn't mind? Terrible twos, screams and all?"

"I raised five hellions. I think I can handle it," she said serenely. "I have Adam's kids on Tuesday afternoons. He'll have fun with them."

Elle reached through the seats and wrapped her arm around her mom's neck. "I don't even care that you called me a hellion when I was totally innocent. You are the very best mom in the whole wide world. I love you."

"She wasn't a hellion," Dad defended her. "She was my pretty little princess."

Elle grinned and turning the other way she kissed her dad on the cheek. "I love you, too."

"It says something, doesn't it—" hope filled Becca's voice "—that he trusts you with his son."

Elle gave a long-suffering laugh. "Good try, Mom. Not going to happen."

"Okay." Her mom sighed. "But it's a shame."

"Why is that?" Elle was almost afraid to ask.

"As Dad says, you were his pretty little princess. As a little girl you spent hours playing Belle. I can just see the two of you together, Beauty and The Beast."

Elle nearly choked on the moisture stick she was using on her lips. People really had to stop saying that.

Later that week Max made his way through the silent arena. Elle had texted him to say she'd commandeered an empty suite to watch the game so Troy could stretch out on the couch when he fell asleep.

It had been a tough week adjusting to being a full-time dad. Surprisingly rewarding, but equally exhausting. He was grateful to Elle's mom for watching Troy during the day and to Elle for helping out during the games.

Donna had returned only to pack her things and fly back to Las Vegas for good. She and Troy had had a good visit and Max had dropped her at the airport this morning. Max was happy for her.

Right behind Elle's text was one from his investigator telling him Amber was on the move. And finally there'd been a voice mail from Amber saying she was back and ready to pick up Troy. She'd be waiting for him at his place.

Not only no, but hell no. Not going to happen.

If he had his way, he'd cut all ties with her, but she was Troy's mother. Max wasn't such a jerk daddy he'd deny his son access to his mother. But it would be on Max's terms.

He reached the suite, opened the door and came to a dead stop. Elle sat on the couch with Troy in her lap, snuggled against her chest. They were both asleep. The domestic scene tugged at something elemental deep in his chest.

How telling that he'd seen more affection and caring in Elle's attitude with Troy than he'd ever seen in Amber's.

Why couldn't Amber be more like Elle?

The unexpected urge to wrap them both up in his arms and hold them close made him hesitate. He didn't do cuddly. Hell, this whole parenting thing was outside his comfort zone.

Elle had warned him he'd have to push himself.

Taking a quiet moment to hold a hot woman in his arms hardly seemed a chore. So it included his kid. Deb would say new experiences were good for his soul.

Willing to put off the confrontation with his baby mama—let Amber see how it felt to wait on someone—he dropped his gear bag and settled into the corner of the couch, carefully pulling Elle into his arms. She fitted perfectly.

At the change of position Troy lifted his head. He blinked at Max, smiled and went back to sleep.

No screams.

The silent acceptance brought a lump to Max's throat. It was a gift, one Max had rarely received. He let out a deep breath and relaxed for the first time in an overly long day.

He drew in the scent of cherry blossoms and…popcorn? Smiling, he eased back into the corner and closed his eyes. He savored the peaceful moment before the approaching storm.

It always surprised him how comfortable he found it to be around Elle.

"Good game," a sleepy voice said softly.

He shifted, drew her closer. "We lost."

"Yes, but it was hard-fought. You only lost by one goal. It's the best the team has played together since Ian was injured."

He ran his thumb over the soft skin of her throat. "Coach asked me to be the interim captain until Ian comes back."

Her chin lifted and she looked at him through lush black lashes. "I can see that."

He grunted. "I can't."

"So you have no opinion about how the team is doing? No thoughts on how it can be improved?"

"I didn't say that." He did have ideas actually. Had been playing around with a bait-and-switch play.

"So you're interested?"

"Now you're baiting me." They really should get going, but he had no desire to move, especially considering what waited for him at home.

"You do remember I just brought Troy to live with me. You're the one talking to me about quality time."

"You're a smart guy." She yawned delicately. "You can handle both."

"You think so?" He had to admit her confidence in him felt good. Having her support surprised him. He'd thought she would want him to put his commitment to Troy first. Instead she thought he could do it all.

He didn't doubt his ability to lead the team. But it did stretch his comfort zone. On the ice he was totally a part of the team. In the locker room he tended to sit back and observe, then go his own way. If he took this on, he'd have to change his ways. Then again, lately he'd been doing a lot of things he didn't normally do.

Like sitting here talking to Elle about his feelings. Had he once wondered what he'd talk to her about? Apparently there was nothing he wouldn't yammer on to her about.

Because that bothered him, he took Troy from her and pushed to his feet. Reaching for her hand, he pulled her up, too.

"It's bad timing," he said.

"It is, but life is rarely convenient. And with that, I have to go."

"Wait." He tightened his hold on her hand. "I heard from Amber."

"What?" she said, forgetting to lower her voice. The exclamation caused Troy to stir. His tiny brow wrinkled, displaying his displeasure. Elle rubbed his back and he relaxed.

"Tell me," she demanded.

"She's back," he told her, referring to Amber. "She said she'd be waiting for me when I got to my place."

"Oh, joy."

"Said she wants to pick up Troy."

"That's it? No explanation? No apology?"

"No. I know her plan. She'll play dumb, then innocent, and finally she'll be all repentant."

"Quite the repertoire." Elle gathered her purse, a computer bag and Troy's backpack.

"She knows all the tricks." Max looped the strap of his gear bag over his free shoulder and held the door for her.

She flipped out the lights. He got another whiff of cherries when she strode by him.

"Do you ever—" She broke off and, shaking her head, took off down the dim corridor.

With his longer stride he quickly caught up to her. "I know exactly what I saw in her, and it sure wasn't mother material. I don't do relationships." He hit the down button for the elevator. The doors opened and they stepped inside.

"How—" She stopped again, eyed him strangely. "You're the last person I would think of to get caught in a situation like this."

"Thanks. I think." They arrived at the bottom floor and he motioned her ahead of him toward the outside doors. She stepped through then held the door for him. The air fogged with their breaths, and a brisk wind held the smell of the nearby ocean. Elle pulled a blanket from Troy's backpack and tossed it over the sleeping boy. They both started up the ramp toward team parking.

"We'd had an important loss," Max heard himself say. "I'd played badly. Stupid story short, I drank more than usual, she was pretty and more than willing to help me forget. We used condoms, yet she still got pregnant."

"I guess it happens."

"I've never told anyone but Harold this, but I think she wanted to get pregnant, that she sabotaged the condoms." Where did that come from? He was a regular blabbermouth tonight.

She froze midstride. He swung around to find an appalled expression on her face and sympathy in her eyes.

"I'm sorry if that's true." She squeezed his arm. "People shouldn't play with other people's lives. She deliberately targeted you?"

He lifted a shoulder, let it drop. "My feeling is that any player would have done. Some people believe I got what I deserved." He started walking again, but got only a few paces when her hand on his arm stopped him.

"They're wrong. Is it a pretty story? No. Is it real? Yes. Regardless, nobody deserves to have their life toyed with."

He stared into her earnest gaze. "Thank you for that." He'd stopped caring what people thought of him a long time ago, but he appreciated her faith in him. "Come home with me."

She blinked at him, her pretty brow pulled into a delicate frown. "What?"

Realizing she was shivering, he took her elbow and led her toward their vehicles.

"I don't want her upsetting Troy. Can you follow me and take him to his room, stay with him?"

"I can take him to my place," she offered without hesitation. "Keep him for tonight."

"No, I want him with me."

"Okay, I'll follow you." Again no hesitation.

"Hmm." He hummed his thanks, tucked her into her car, buckled Troy into his seat and drove home carefully keeping track of Elle in his rearview mirror.

Predictably, Amber was parked in the middle of the driveway, leaving him and Elle to park on the street.

He lifted a sleeping Troy into his arms, then met Elle and walked up the drive, deliberately putting her on his side away from Amber.

"It's about time," Amber said, climbing from her car. Moonlight shone off her long blond hair. She wore a tiny black dress and impossibly high heels. Beautiful as always, but it was all on the surface. "It's been over an hour. You could have hurried knowing I was waiting."

Ignoring her, Max continued to the door and slid his key into the lock. Inside, he handed Troy off to Elle. "Thanks."

"Hold it." Amber jumped in front of Elle, her impressive cleavage bouncing. "He's going with me."

Max inserted himself between the women. "No. He's not. Elle, take him upstairs."

She tried to move around them and again Amber shifted, blocking her way. "That's my son, bitch. You're not taking him anywhere."

Max advanced to tower over her. "Apologize to my friend or this conversation is already over."

"Max." She petted him, pretending affection. "Don't be that way. I was a bad girl." She simpered, turning his stomach with her false show of intimacy. "You made me wait—isn't that punishment enough?"

"You were inconvenienced a few minutes," he sneered as he stepped away from her. "What about the people you've left waiting for days?" He saw Troy starting to stir and motioned for Elle to go on.

Amber saw the gesture. She seemed to realize if Troy got away from her now, she'd lose any chance of taking him with her. Smart of her, because she was right.

"I don't think so." She sidestepped, blocking Elle's exit again. "He's coming with me. Come to Mama, Troy." She tried to take the toddler.

"Stay away." Elle turned, using her elbow to protect Troy from the other woman.

"Max, tell your girlfriend to give me my son before I hurt her."

"I'm not his—"

"Don't pretend you don't know what's happening here, Amber," Max derided, cutting Elle off. Wanting to deflect Amber's attention from Elle, he gently took Troy. He met Elle's questioning gaze. "Thanks," he whispered.

To Amber he said, "I haven't heard an apology. It's time for you to leave."

"I'm not leaving without Troy." She crossed her arms over her chest, plumping up her breasts. It just served to make her look desperate.

"Mama?" Troy blinked and rubbed his eyes. He made no move toward his mother. His eyes closed over again.

Elle stepped to his side, placed her hand on Troy's back. "If you care anything for him," she said, "you'll leave before you upset him."

"Bitch." Amber's arm swung and her hand connected with Elle's cheek. "Don't tell me how to be with my son." She turned a ferocious glare on Max. "Troy is my son. I won't give him up without a fight or a big check."

Before he could think, before Amber stopped talking, Elle reacted. She stepped forward and grabbed Amber's hand.

"You will apologize, now," Elle said.

"Go to hell." Amber tried to pull away and flinched. "Let go."

"No." Her cheek an angry red, Elle smiled for all she was worth. "It'll only hurt if you struggle. Your son is half-awake, so your little tantrum is over."

"Elle."

"No, Max." She never looked at him as she turned with Amber toward the door. "This is between us women. I have four brothers," she whispered to Amber, "all much bigger and stronger than you, and all have hit their knees when I use this hold. My daddy taught it to me. Now smile so Troy knows everything is okay, and then say you're sorry."

Max should step in, but Elle had things handled, and the way he felt, her approach was much gentler than his would be.

Amber sent Elle a venomous glare and opened her mouth.

Elle must not have liked what she saw in Amber's expression. She smiled sweetly and tightened her grip.

"Sorry!" Amber gasped. "I'm sorry. And I'm leaving. Let go."

"Say bye-bye to Troy," Elle demanded.

"'Bye, Troy." Amber glared at Elle, snatching her hand back when Elle released her at the front door. She barely glanced at Troy, who'd fallen back asleep. "Mama will see you soon."

Elle reached for the doorknob and pointedly held the door open wide. "Don't make promises you can't keep."

Amber stepped over the threshold and turned back, her glance targeting him. "Max," she implored him.

The door shut in her face.

Max advanced on Elle, watched the expressions flicker

across her face: satisfaction, chagrin, regret and pain as she touched her cheek.

He took her hand, kissed the palm. "Are you okay?"

"I will be." She attempted a smile, grimaced instead. "I'm sorry if I overstepped myself, but instinct took over. As the only girl in a houseful of boys, I learned to defend myself. And you did tell her to go."

"Let me kiss it better." He lowered his head, gently pressed his mouth to her cheek. "You are so hot."

"Ha." She gave a surprised laugh. "Fool."

"Sexy." He feathered his lips to hers, kissed her softly. "I feel so safe."

Laughing out loud, she shook her head. And then he watched in horror as a flood of tears filled her brown eyes. Blinking frantically, she turned away and swiped at her cheeks.

"Hey, whoa." He wrapped an arm around her and pulled her back against his chest. "Don't cry. You're okay. We're all okay. Because of you."

"I'm sorry. I'm being silly."

"She hurt you." In his house. Impotent rage flowed through his blood. But he held it in check, for her.

"Yes. No. It's not that." Her breath hitched. "Troy."

He sighed, glancing down at Troy. He was asleep against Max's shoulder. His mother's appearance hadn't been enough to fully penetrate his sleep.

"Troy will be fine," he told her, hoping he spoke the truth. In bringing Elle home with him Max had hoped to spare Troy a nasty scene. Instead it had only made it worse. "If anyone should apologize, it's me. Or Amber. She's the one who got violent. You were subtlety in action."

"Daddy." Troy patted Max's cheek without opening his eyes. "Night-night."

At the sound of Troy's voice she turned in Max's arms. With a last swipe at her eyes, she focused her attention on the boy.

"He's right. Time for him to be in bed." She glanced at Max through her lashes. "Need help?"

"I won't say no."

"Mama bye-bye?" Troy asked sleepily. He lifted his head from Max's shoulder and blinked at him.

"Yes. Mama went bye-bye," Max confirmed. He looked into Elle's brown eyes. "She outstayed her welcome as soon as she insulted you."

"Maybe I should go," she whispered.

"No." He wasn't ready for her to leave. Didn't want the scene with Amber to be what she left here with.

Wrapping a hand around the back of her head he held her still and claimed her mouth in a sensual kiss. Her warm response was immediate and erotic. She opened to him, shifted closer, invited him in. He deepened the embrace, enjoying the feel of her, the taste of her, the heat of her.

Breathing hard he pulled back, pressed his forehead to hers. "Stay."

"We shouldn't," she denied, passion making her voice husky.

"Stay anyway."

CHAPTER NINE

STAY. HE SAID IT so easily.

And oh, he tempted her so.

Being held tight against his hard, strong body just added to the juice already revving through her system. The encounter with the she-witch had been both appalling and exhilarating.

The problem was that the mix of passion and adrenaline just served to muddle her thinking. She and Max were supposed to be at odds, downright hostile. But as the week advanced she'd found her emotions changing. Which was totally disconcerting.

The whole situation left her feeling queasy, like she used to when she was a kid and she felt out of control. But no matter how she tried to organize her feelings, they refused to be categorized into a neat little box.

At the same time, she'd never felt so alive, so drawn to another person.

So when he tugged on her fingers, she went.

"Okay," she submitted on a rush of desire, "but I'm going on record that this is a very bad idea."

He stopped and swooped in for another kiss. "It'll be worth it. Because I have the feeling being with you will be very, very good."

She blinked at him. "Let's put Troy to bed."

He grinned, his dimple flashing rakishly. Her knees melted and, that easily, all reservations vanished. She was so lost.

Together they got Troy ready for bed: she stripped him down while Max gathered the boy's pajamas and the nighttime pull-ons Troy used.

Max took every opportunity to amp her already tingling body. A rub of his hand here, a sniff of her hair there, caging her against the changing table so his body touched hers everywhere. It was distracting, tantalizing, thrilling.

The boy slept through it all.

"Can you hurry?" Max whispered against her neck, his breath warm on the exposed skin. Longing shivered down her spine.

"Behave." She arched her neck, giving him better access even as she sought something to sidetrack him. "I see you made some changes in here."

"Took me a while but I finally converted the crib into a bed. The bedding is what you bought."

"And your hockey stuff." Posters, an old hockey stick and puck, along with a framed jersey decorated the walls. "It looks great."

"The jersey is my first with a professional team. The Anaheim Ducks."

"I'm sure he loves it." The jersey was the retro colors of orange, black and gold, which went well with the muted beige and brown, red and blue of the five-sport bedding set she'd picked up while shopping with Michelle.

"I know I love it when he's in bed." He swung Troy into his arms and carried him to the bed.

She pulled the covers back and Max settled the boy on his pillow. He looked so tiny, so sweet, sleeping in his big-boy bed. She tucked him in and kissed his cheek, then watched as Max did the same.

When he stood up, she wrapped her arms around his neck, looked into his eyes. "He's gotten to you, hasn't he?"

"He's cool for a kid." Hands on her waist he walked her toward the door. "What do you expect, he's my son."

"Softy."

"Watch it. I have a reputation to consider." In the hall he pulled the door closed behind them. Drawing her close he lowered his head and opened his lips over hers. That quickly, her nerves ignited, sending tingles sizzling to her pulse points.

"Last chance to change your mind," he said against her mouth. "Once we get to my room, there's no turning back."

He didn't fool her—all she had to do was say no and he'd stop. She knew that about him. He was a man of honor and strength, of restraint and surprising modesty. He'd fallen for his son, and she was falling for him. Hard.

She should walk away. That would be the smart thing to do. Safer for her heart and her career. But in this moment all she wanted were his arms around her, his hands and mouth making her feel alive, desired, loved.

Lifting onto her toes, she buried her fingers in his short, soft hair, holding him in place while she bit his lip then soothed the nip with her tongue.

He groaned, angled his head to snag her mouth again and deepened the kiss, telling her with his actions how much he wanted her.

He swung her up into his arms and lifted his head long enough to say, "I'll take that as a yes."

In his room he laid her on the bed, followed her down. The weight of him felt so good. She clutched him to her, trailed kisses down his neck, arched into him when his fingers found a sweet spot.

Humming his approval he stroked her again then worked his hand under her blouse, lifting the garment up and over her head.

"Yes!" She immediately went at the buttons on his shirt and it became a frantic tussle as they fought to rid each other of their clothes. Finally skin met skin, mouth melded to mouth, body shaped to body, and still she strained to get closer.

"You like that?" A smile formed against her temple before his tongue sampled her in a heated caress.

"More." She wallowed in him, his scent, his touch, his taste. Everything male about him appealed, excited, satisfied everything female in her. She loved the feel of him under her fingers, running her hands over his skin, finding the different textures, smooth, hair-roughened, soft, tough, thrilling to his sensual response as she explored each new territory in depth.

And he returned the favor. A true combatant, he approached lovemaking with a strategy designed to assess, weaken and overcome. And he was every bit as masterful in bed as he was on the ice.

The man knew how to use his hands.

He assessed with gentle intensity, weakened with tender demand and overcame with erotic insistence, claiming all of her until she surrendered both mind and body to his carnal assault.

She gave everything asked of her, and in return she turned his passion back on him, bringing him with her to a shattering culmination.

Max stared at the ceiling, striving for inspiration. Making love to Elle ranked as one of the best times of his life.

Right up there with winning the Stanley Cup with the Ducks.

The win had been the first for the Ducks, the first for a California team. He hoped to bring the same luck to San Diego. Hopefully this year.

Until tonight nothing had beat the high of that win.

The problem was he wanted to keep her.

He pressed his nose to her hair, inhaled cherries and smiled. The sense of belonging he experienced in her arms went beyond anything he'd ever known. Ever hoped to know.

And it had started nearly a year ago. Dancing in the moonlight, holding her close, falling into her kiss. He'd stolen that time, let the magic carry him away for an hour. But in the end he'd known being with her was a fantasy he could never have.

Now he struggled between believing what they had was too good to be true, and finding a way to claim her as his. Honestly, he just wanted to wake her and make her his all over again.

Instead he kissed her hair and stole quietly from the bed. Pulling on his shorts he let himself out of the room. On his way downstairs he checked on Troy. He had the baby monitors, but preferred to do a visual check when he was up.

Troy slept peacefully. Max would like him some of that. Since it wasn't coming, he skipped down the stairs and made his way to the living room and the grand piano. He flexed his fingers, ran them down the keys and back, then began a classical piece.

The strength and power of the music appealed to him. Playing fed his soul but also freed his mind to ponder.

He solved a lot of his problems in this seat.

All he came up with tonight was the realization that timing sucked.

Elle's passion, her support over the past week even when she clearly disapproved of him, her affection for Troy, had won him over.

Generally he had no problem breaking a few rules, but if he took on the role of captain, as he was being urged to do, he'd need to curb that tendency. Plus Amber was about to make his life a living hell.

Elle deserved better than to be dragged through the stink with him. She'd literally put her life on hold to help him. And he hadn't made it easy for her.

Shame on him.

He was paying for it now. He'd finally found a woman he had feelings for, and he was the worst thing that could happen to her. Being with him was a threat to her career and her reputation.

No way was he going to let Amber bring Elle down with him.

His reputation could take it. He was The Beast, people practically expected bad behavior from him. And she'd done her best to put his relationship with Troy into a good light.

He'd known a lot of women, but this was the first time his gut had gotten involved, the first time he felt the promise of something more. He liked her. Her courage, her competitiveness. Her loyalty.

For a minute there he'd thought she was going to nail Amber with a right hook. But Elle thought before she acted. Something he truly admired as it was a self-taught talent he still struggled with.

He had no doubt she could have clocked Amber. All without putting a hair out of place on her own head, thanks to the education of her four older brothers.

Max reached for his phone, realized he'd left it up-stairs and made a mental note to send the Austin family box seats for a game. He owed them for the experience of watching Elle frog-walk Amber to his front door.

What a woman.

The scene had made him so hot. He'd longed to wrap her in his arms right then, right there. And he would have except for the need to take care of his child first. That she helped Max put Troy to bed with tender affection tinged with heated feminine urgency had just made Max hotter to have her.

And wow! Amazing what liking a woman added to the experience.

Freaked him out a little. No, it freaked him out a lot.

But he was no coward. He wanted to spend time with her, see where this thing between them was going.

Feathering his fingers over the keys, he built the momentum, holding his posture as he sped from note to note, pounding faster and faster until he reached the crescendo.

There was just one big problem. In protecting him and Troy, Elle had made an enemy of Amber. Max couldn't let Elle get hurt. Not because of him.

He was used to loneliness, to handling things alone, on his own terms. He should have stuck with that model and not involved the team or anyone else.

He'd been thinking he might be able to save his career if he had the team working with him, backing him on this whole parenting gig. And they'd really stepped up. Elle was solid as a rock and Ray hadn't hesitated, blustered a bit, but he'd come through.

Amber knew how to work the angles; she had contacts in the press that would listen to her. No matter that what she spat out was half truths at best and more often than not outright lies, her contacts didn't care. The more sensational the headline the better they liked it, and it was up to the victim to prove it wasn't the truth.

Elle wanted a career in public relations. She knew how it worked. Knew, too, that being connected to something like this could be a career wrecker.

"You play the piano?" There was surprise in the sleep-husky voice.

He looked up at her, and took a fist to the heart. Dressed in one of his shirts held together by a single button, her hair a wild mess of curls, she took his breath away.

She walked over on bare feet to sit next to him on the bench. "I thought this was just a showpiece."

"That's what most people think." He settled his hands on the keys, the instrument falling silent.

"Don't stop," she urged him. "I like it, though I wouldn't have pegged you for classical."

He chose a lighter sonata, started picking it out. "I like the classics, and, yeah, I know I'm butchering it."

"No. It's lovely." She inched closer, her arm stealing around his waist, but she stayed behind him allowing him the freedom to play. "Who taught you?"

"Deb turned me on to it. Taught me a few pieces. I've taught myself the rest. I also like jazz and hard rock. But when I play I lean toward the classics. The power and depth appeals to me."

"You taught yourself? I'm impressed."

"The first thing I did when I got picked up by the Ducks was buy Deb and Pat season tickets to the symphony. She loved it. She refused to take them after Pat died, so I bought them for me and gave them to her to hold. When I'm in town, we go together. If I'm out of town, she takes a friend."

"That's very sweet." She sighed. "I love jazz. A good

saxophone piece can touch your soul. Do you know what I mean?"

Max nodded, and let the tension ease from his shoulders. She wasn't going to laugh. At his playing. Or at him.

He caressed the keys, giving her his favorite jazz piece. "I heard this in New York at the Beacon Theatre."

"Oh! I'm so jealous." She squeezed his arm. "I bet you could get backstage."

His head shook in automatic reaction to her question. "I never go backstage."

"Why not?" she demanded, obviously outraged on behalf of everyone who would like to go backstage and couldn't. "Are you embarrassed to be caught enjoying music?"

"No." He couldn't look at her. Embarrassment had nothing to do with his feelings. He loved the music, but sometimes he sat in the dark and felt like a fraud. It was so beautiful, so cultured, and he was just a punk from the streets. "It's private," he told her, hoping it would suffice. "Something I do for me."

"Humph." She still sounded disgruntled. "Figures. And here I was planning a night at the symphony for my nephew's team. It would be so good for boys to see their sports heroes enjoying a little culture. I swear I've spent half my life looking for a man who understands there are enjoyable pursuits in life beyond sports."

Now he did look at her, admired the way the light filtering from the kitchen caught the gleam in her fiery hair. Had she just admitted he was her dream man?

Nah. Having something in common didn't make them soul mates.

"A lot of men go for the arts."

"Yes, and they are perfectly nice men."

"But?"

"Nothing." She gave a casual shrug, causing the collar of his shirt to slide off her creamy shoulder.

He simply lifted one dark eyebrow.

She bit her lip, holding back for all of a minute before blurting, "But boring." Rolling her eyes in self-disgust, she spilled, "Most of my life revolves around sports. My family are big-time sports people, my job is sports-related—"

"Why?" he broke in. "If you find sports so overwhelming, why work for a professional sports team?"

"Simple. It's what I know. I wasn't into sports myself but my family was, so I focused on the business side. I worked my way through college as assistant to the athletic director at State and when I graduated he recommended me to the Thunder team. It was a great opportunity. But what I really want is my own business. I'd like to work with foundations to help make a difference in the world."

"Admirable." He wondered what she'd say if she knew he funded a foundation to help keep kids off the street. It was something so private, so personal, he found it hard to talk about. For the first time he was tempted to share.

"You can see why I want something more in my private life than someone looking for the next game."

And the moment passed.

"Shouldn't be so hard to find."

"You wouldn't think so, huh? But it's my experience men either like sports or the arts. Few straddle the line."

"A smart man would adjust simply for the opportunity to straddle you." He turned toward her, lifting one leg up and over the bench so she sat between the spread of his legs. Seeing the bruise on her cheek, knowing he was in part to blame, sickened him. Tomorrow he'd deal with that. Now he leaned close and ran his tongue the length of her neck.

"I think I need my shirt back."

Delicate fingers cupped his cheek and she kissed him softly, making him ache from the sweetness of her taste.

"You are wicked," she admonished him.

"Well, I am The Beast." He growled low in his throat then took a nip of that creamy shoulder. "And I'm not done with you yet."

"Good." Melting against him, she looped her arms around his neck. "Because I'm not done with you either."

Wrapping an arm around her waist he pulled her into him, letting her feel how much he wanted her. Damn her dream man. He might be her future. Tonight belonged to Max.

He wouldn't put her through the media circus to come. Having her by his side throughout the ordeal was nothing more than a fantasy. And he'd learned a long time ago to deal in reality.

If he lost his career over this, he'd survive it. If he cost her her career, he'd never forgive himself.

It might not be too late. If he created distance between them, it might be enough to keep her from becoming collateral damage to his domestic nightmare.

So yes, he'd give her up, but not tonight. He lifted her into his arms and carried her to the couch. Tonight she was his to cherish, his to adore. With a groan he sank into her welcoming arms and let the world fade away.

Elle woke with a smile. She felt good. Better than good. She felt energized, satisfied and surprisingly rested. Surprisingly because of the lack of sleep.

She stretched and her body hummed with contentment. An emotion that stayed even when she opened her eyes and found herself back in Max Beasley's bed. She remembered every scorching moment of the night before.

Reaching out for Max and encountering only cool

sheets motivated her to prop up on her elbows and sur-
vey the room. No sign of him. Her mood dimmed a bit.

And then she noticed full sunlight hit the east-facing
window, filling the room with warmth and light. Uh-oh.
No. The clock read 8:45 a.m.

"Max," she called out as she swung the covers back
and hopped from the bed.

No response from the man, but baby sounds came from
the monitor. Troy was here, which surely meant Max was
somewhere in the house. Probably making coffee.

She could really use some coffee.

She grabbed up her clothes—where were her panties?—and dodged into the shower. When she stepped
out eight minutes later, Troy's cries streamed through the
monitor and there was still no sign of Max. Or her panties.

Giving up on her underwear she hurried into her
clothes and went after Troy.

"Hey, babe." She smiled at the cranky toddler. "Good
morning."

"Elle." He scrambled off the bed and flew across the
room.

She swooped him up and cuddled him close. Poor baby,
tears stained his cheeks. She should have checked on him
before taking her shower, but she'd been sure Max would
get him. Now, not so sure. And a sinking feeling began
to grow within her.

Last night had been magical. She'd known, of course,
that it meant nothing, that it was just two people scratch-
ing an itch. She'd told herself she could handle the casual
night of loving.

After all, she'd gotten over her major objections to
the man.

His arrogance hid a surprising vulnerability that came
from his dysfunctional childhood. Which made his de-

termined dedication to Troy all the more admirable as he strove to give his child something he'd clearly lacked himself.

She had so lied to herself.

And that wasn't the biggest mistake she'd made.

Oh, it had started out casually enough. Fueled by adrenaline and desire, that first time had been hot and fast, totally hormone-driven. But after finding him at the piano, finding they shared a love of music, she'd experienced a closeness that transcended a casual joining.

And that next time he'd been carnal, and yes, totally wicked, but also tender, his touch so reverent she lost a little of her soul.

Now he was missing in action. So not good.

She prayed he hadn't built her up just to leave her. Again.

She headed downstairs in search of her errant lover. If they'd been at her house, she could see him making a dawn escape. But this was his place. And even if he'd felt compelled to bypass the morning-after confrontation, he wouldn't have just left Troy behind. Would he?

Obviously he would. She found the note propped against the coffee machine. Short and to the point, no salutation, no signature.

Had an early meeting.
Can you drop Troy at your mom's?

She crushed the note in a clenched fist. It shouldn't hurt so much. But it did. It was a slap to the face when she'd allowed herself to hope for more. Big mistake. Huge. She couldn't believe she'd let him reject her again.

Well, message received loud and clear.

"Daddy?" Troy asked.

"Daddy went bye-bye," she said through a clogged throat. "Come on, baby." She settled him more comfortably on her hip. "Let's get you ready to go."

"Juice?"

"I'll get you something on the road," she promised.

She needed out of this house now.

CHAPTER TEN

MAX HUFFED INTO his cupped hands, warming his fingers with the heat of his breath. Clouds hung heavy in a gray sky as a brisk wind shook palm fronds and blew the dew across his windshield.

He sat in his SUV outside his own home feeling like a complete jerk. Probably because he *was* a jerk.

Regardless, he'd stay until he saw Elle leave.

Though he'd been sitting here a while and had seen no sign of Amber, he didn't trust her not to accost Elle again. Not to make another try for Troy.

Unwilling to risk either option he waited and watched to make sure Elle left safely. And to make sure she'd gotten his silent message: last night meant nothing.

And then the door opened and he saw her. His heart kicked up a gear. She was so beautiful, the radiance of her red hair warming him in lieu of the missing sunshine.

By the very way she moved—short crisp steps, her body nearly brittle with the stiffness of her posture—he knew he'd hit the mark with his note. Damn.

He'd meant to push her away, but he took no satisfaction in hurting her.

Nothing in his life—having no parents, rotting in the system, living on the streets—none of it had been harder than pulling away from the warm haven of his bed this morning.

Max didn't whine about his life. It was what it was. He barely remembered his folks—instead he recalled the pain and fear of a three-year-old suddenly alone in the world, and the loneliness that followed. He'd hated growing up in the system, knowing the check that came with him was more important than he was. He lasted thirteen years before he took off and made his way west.

Living on the streets made foster care look good.

He swiped at the condensation on the window, pushing the memories away as he focused on the woman across the way. Even hurting, she handled the boy with affection and care. She competently strapped him into his seat and from where Max sat, half a block away, he heard his son laugh.

Everything about Elle fitted him, from the feel of her in his arms, to her get-it-done attitude, to her tenderness for Troy and her feisty competitiveness. And yeah, in spite of her resentment of sports ruling her childhood, that was something that ran true in her family. He loved that about her.

Wait. No. He didn't do love.

Sure this thing with Elle had potential. But it wasn't love. He didn't know how to love. He liked being with her, liked the man he was when he spent time with her. And yeah, she made him yearn for things he'd never had.

But now wasn't the time to think of himself.

He owed it to Troy to provide a safe, stable home for him. The boy deserved to know a sense of security, of unconditional love. Max truly wanted to give his son the home he'd never known.

Already the boy thrived in his care. Troy laughed easily, talked more. And most telling of all, he'd stopped screaming.

Elle had helped them make it to this point. He owed her. He might be a jerk, but this was for her own good. She was everything that was bright and open and beautiful. He'd do everything in his power to protect her from the ugliness that was Amber.

He'd put up with Amber's antics because she was Troy's mother and he'd felt he owed his son a little tolerance. For Elle he'd do what he hadn't been willing to do for himself.

He slid open his phone and hit the number for his investigator.

"Max." A deep voice came on the line. "I thought I might hear from you."

"Send me everything you have on her," Max ordered. "I need leverage."

"I'll drop it off this afternoon."

"I want someone on her 24/7," Max demanded. "And I want to know immediately if she goes anywhere near Elle Austin."

On her way to her parents' house, Elle pulled into a fast-food drive-through and picked up an egg-and-sausage sandwich and a hash-brown patty she shared with Troy. An orange juice for him and coffee for her rounded out the order. Not the breakfast of champions, but today it would have to do.

She flipped off the radio, unable to take the Christmas carols, all joyful and bright. Her mood couldn't take the happiness and she really didn't need the reminder of the approaching holiday. Or the reminder of what a fool she'd been at last year's Gala, which had only been practice for this year's idiocy.

At her mom's she pasted on a smile and carried Troy inside. Please let this be a quick in-and-out.

Luck was not with her. Troy scurried off to the toy bin in the corner of the family room, but her mom took one look at Elle and demanded to know what was wrong.

"Come with me." Becca towed Elle into the kitchen, which opened onto the family room so they could keep an eye on Troy, and pushed her into a chair at the table. "Talk to me."

"Sorry, Mom. I can't today." Elle immediately pushed to her feet and leaned over to give her mom a kiss. "We'll catch up soon. I promise."

Becca's arm shot out, blocking Elle's exit. "Sit down, young lady."

"I'm not a teenager anymore, Mom," Elle protested. "I have a job and responsibilities."

"Yes, and I'm helping out with one of those responsibilities," Becca reminded her. "That should earn me a few minutes of your time." Standing, she held Elle at arm's length, her touch familiar and comforting. "Is it Max?"

How did she do that? Of course she nailed it in one guess.

"Why would you think that?" She knew her mother harbored hopes for Elle to settle into a committed relationship, but her mother knew how she felt about sportsmen, so she couldn't imagine Max inspiring much optimism in that regard.

"Perhaps because you couldn't take your eyes off each other during Walter's party? You can fool a lot of people, kiddo, but not me. It was clear the chemistry between you wasn't all hostility."

"You are so wrong." Elle sank back into her seat. "He's done nothing but use me. And that ends today."

"Oh, baby. You've fallen for him, haven't you?"

"No." Instant denial rolled off her tongue. Then she

threw herself down and knocked her head on the table repeatedly. "Yes. How could I be such a fool?"

"Honey, love makes fools of all of us at some point."

"Not helpful, Mom."

"How about this—I saw the way he looked at you, how he stepped forward to protect you. Believe me, he's not a disinterested party."

"It's not personal. That's just how he is. He cares more than people give him credit for. He's smart and competitive and he's really trying with Troy. But—" she shook her head "—so damaged. I don't think he can let a woman close."

"I'm telling you, you aren't in this alone. Have a little patience. Everything that's going on with Troy must have Max tied in knots right now. I'm sure he's a little defensive, a little leery."

"Oh yeah. Hot and cold." If Elle put her hurt aside, she supposed dealing with Amber could trigger evasive-action tendencies.

"Exactly. He made a life-altering mistake. Yes, it gave him Troy, but right now that just doubles the ramifications of future mistakes."

"And I'm a future mistake." Last night hadn't felt like a mistake, but this morning, sitting at her mom's table in yesterday's clothes—sans panties—felt a whole lot different.

"I'm not saying that." Becca put the back of her hand against Elle's brow. "Are you feeling okay? Your cheeks just went bloodred."

Ducking away from her mom's hand, Elle crossed her legs.

"He plays the piano, a beautiful grand piano that he has in his living room." She lifted stark eyes and met her mother's concerned gaze. "He has season tickets to the symphony."

"Oh, baby." Understanding softened Becca's eyes as she tucked a piece of hair behind Elle's ear.

"And the thing is it didn't even matter. I fell for him before I knew of his love for music. I'm so doomed."

"I know you like to have everything organized and orderly, but love is messy. I urge you to embrace the experience. Don't shut him out when he may need you most."

"What about what I need? Doesn't that count?"

"Of course you matter. I want you to be happy more than anything in the world. But the truth is you come from a loving family. For all you've been focused on your career instead of finding a husband, you know what love is. You're capable of opening your heart to someone. From what you say, Max hasn't known a lot of love in his life. It may not be a matter of he can't let anyone close as much as he doesn't know how."

Max stepped out of Coach's office from the first of the many meetings he'd committed to as the interim captain and ran into Hank and Jaden in the hall.

"Max." Hank raised his hand for a high five. "Heard the news, man, congratulations. The team is in good hands."

"They got the wrong man, if you ask me," Jaden declared. "They should have asked me."

"Maybe in ten years," Max responded, unoffended. "Once you've chipped off some of that ego."

"Take note, old man," Jaden scoffed. "It's not ego if you've got the skills."

"Get your stick out of your ass, Jaden. Yeah, you're good, but you're playing with the big boys now. We're all good. So leave your attitude in the locker room because on the ice we're a team."

Jaden puffed up. "Hey, you can't—"

"Yeah, I can." Max calmly cut him off. "Listen, I'm the biggest loner in this pack, but even I know that on the ice we're a team."

"Jaden, bro, you need to hear him." Hank shuffled his big body from foot to foot.

Resistance shouted from Jaden's towering frame.

Max stayed in control. "Do you want the Stanley Cup or not?"

Jaden gave a sharp nod. "You know it."

"Well, you can't get it alone. The team needs your mind on the game, not hotshotting. If you can't do that, Bates can."

"Bates? He's older than you!"

"He's a solid player and puts the team first. And that will be my recommendation to Coach." Max glanced at his watch. "On the ice in twenty. Come to win."

"Elle, you're off the Beasley issue." Ray stood in her office doorway later that morning. "Meeting for the Wish upon a Puck Gala, my office, thirty minutes."

"Wait." She hurried after him. "What do you mean I'm off the Beasley issue? Why?"

"He said he doesn't need any more help." He kept walking.

Elle caught up to him. "But Amber got back last night. She made quite a scene at his place when she tried to take Troy back." Max might be on her hit list but Troy deserved all the protection they could give him. "Now is when he needs us most."

"He says different. And I need your help with the Gala." He stopped, gave her a pat on the arm. "Max said to thank you, Elle, that you did a good job." With that he turned into his office and closed his door.

Elle made her way back to her desk. Sank into her chair. Max had fired her. And then had given her a glowing review. He might as well have written up her pink slip. Because, of course, Ray had to know they'd slept together.

And Max didn't even have the courtesy to tell her to her face.

She shouldn't care. Hadn't wanted to do the job in the first place. But last night had changed things between them. She understood if he didn't want to continue working with her. Making love had crossed a line. But be a man. Have the guts to tell her himself.

But then, he had a history of walking away with no word. She should have known this was where they would end up. But knowing didn't ease the pain. Actually, knowledge made it worse, because the man she'd grown to know wouldn't hurt her in this way.

Which just served to confuse her more.

Putting him from her mind, she brooded for twenty minutes over a press release Jenna had given to her to proof before giving up and heading to Ray's office for the meeting. He looked up with a stern expression and her heart sank into her stomach.

"Close the door," he said.

Not a good sign. She expected others for the meeting so this must be something else. She slid into one of his visitor chairs.

"What's happened?" she demanded. This was no time to go soft.

"I take it you haven't seen the tabloids this morning?" He moved a file and exposed a colorful print magazine.

Her hand shook as she reached for it, so she quickly set it on the desk in front of her. Mortification sliced deep as she read the blaring headline: Beauties Fight Over The Beast.

Amber must have had a photographer with her last night, someone taking pictures through the glass sliding doors of the patio. The photo showed a zoom shot of Amber slapping Elle while Max stood in the background holding Troy. In a smaller shot she and Amber appeared to be struggling.

It was bad, really bad.

She kept her head down, pretending to read while truthfully she couldn't meet Ray's gaze.

She should be fired. Part of her job included watching the tabloids for references to the team or players and letting Ray know so they could get in front of the problem.

Actually appearing in a front-page scandal? There was no excuse, no explanation, that made it all right. Worse, she'd been so caught up in self-pity she hadn't even followed her regular routine and been on top of the mess.

"Ra—" Nothing came out so she cleared her throat, tried again. "Ray, I—"

"Before we go into all that, are you okay?"

Now she couldn't see him for the tears in her eyes. She blinked them back; a professional didn't cry.

"Yes." She found her hand had gone to her sore cheek and she carefully returned it to the desktop. "I'm sorry I wasn't on top of this. We had no idea anyone was with Amber. There were no flashes to signal a photographer was lurking outside. But that's no excuse. I should have checked the tabloids this morning. I'll have my resignation on—"

"What? Whoa." Ray held up a hand, his bushy eyebrows nearly meeting in a scowl. "I don't want to hear anything about a resignation. We knew it would get ugly with Amber, but Max didn't tell me it got physical. No wonder he cut you loose. If he hadn't, I would have pulled you anyway. Now I get why he was so concerned."

"But—"

"No argument, Elle. I won't put you in harm's way."

"I appreciate that, but I actually won that altercation. And Max still needs our help."

"I didn't say we wouldn't continue to help him. The players don't have to ask for the team to help with public relations." Ray considered her and then nodded. "Max will get the help he needs, but it won't be you. Stay clear of him until this blows over. We don't want to give the press anything more to work with."

"That won't be a problem," she assured him whole-heartedly. "His nanny arrives tomorrow."

"Good. Keep your distance." He swept up the tabloid, tapped the picture. "Amber blew it with this picture, shows her as the aggressor. That's a mistake we can capitalize on." He dropped the magazine in a desk drawer and waved to the people waiting in the hall. "Now on to the Gala."

As the room filled with people, Elle sank back in her seat. Keep her distance? Yeah, she could do that.

Right after she reclaimed her panties.

If it was the last thing she did, Elle would hunt Maxwell Beasley down and rip out his heart.

He'd promised Walter he'd come to his hockey practice today, but he was a no-show. Damn him.

She could handle his rejection; she was an adult. Walter was just a boy. He didn't understand Max had better places to be, better people to see.

"I'm sorry, Adam. I should never have brought him to the party."

She stood next to her brother on the sideline in an over-size jersey with her hair tucked up in a Thunders' cap, incognito, in order to speak to the rotter who hadn't both-ered to show. This was the line for her. He could hurt her;

she should have known better than to let him close. But don't mess with her family.

Walter idolized Max without realizing why the man inherited the moniker *The Beast*. Walter was an innocent and it killed her he was being hurt because of her. He deserved so much better.

"Don't sweat it." Adam knocked the bill of her cap down over her eyes. "I'll take them out for pizza. They'll get over it."

She cringed. "So he told the whole team?"

"Of course. They've been talking about it all week."

"I'm going to kill him, you know." She gritted through clenched teeth.

"Like you took on that Amber chick? He should be shaking in his skates."

Oh, no. Already it was starting. She'd fended off calls from each of her brothers this morning, assuring them she was fine and explaining she'd taken care of business. But she knew her brothers, knew if she didn't stop it now, she'd be razzed endlessly about being taken down in front of all America.

So not going to happen.

In no mood to be teased she turned narrowed eyes on him. In a flash she snapped her hand out and grabbed his finger in the dragon-toe grip.

"Ow, ouch." He squirmed next to her, wanting to pull away but knowing it would only make it worse. He gave her a stern look. "Mom said you weren't supposed to use the grip anymore."

"Mom's not here." She squeezed a little harder.

"Okay, okay. Stop." He went still, no longer fighting the grip. "You cleaned house."

"I showed her to the door." Elle released him. "And don't you forget it."

"Respect." He grabbed her in a hug, squeezed hard. "You're sure you weren't hurt? It's a good thing Max isn't here. I'd have to talk to him about how he's handling his women."

She wiggled free, glared up at him. "I'm not one of his women."

"Good— Hey, it's Jaden and Hank from the Thunders." He headed toward the new arrivals. "Guess Max is off the hook since he sent reinforcements."

Slowly following, listening to the squeals of the kids as they caught sight of the professional players, Elle acknowledged it was a good save. And she really hated to give Max any credit while still angry with him.

"Hey, Elle." Hank swept her off her feet in an enthusiastic bear hug. "Max said to tell you he was sorry he couldn't make it."

"I bet." She blew out a breath of relief when her feet hit the floor, and then greeted Jaden. "Slacker," she said of Max. "I appreciate you guys coming out."

"Don't be too hard on him. He wanted to be here," Hank assured her. "But Coach made him interim team captain and Max had to hang back to sit in on some meetings."

So he'd taken on the job. "I'm glad. You sound happy with the decision."

"We are," Hank confirmed. "Max is going to make a stellar captain. The man has more ice smarts than anyone I know."

"And two hat tricks already this season," Jaden added grudgingly.

"I know what a hat trick is," Walter spoke up from where the boys were all lined up against the rink fence gawking at the players. "It's when you get three goals in the same game."

"That's right." Hank stood with his hands in the pockets of his hoodie. "How many hat tricks do you have?"

Walter's smile turned into a frown. "None. I'm the goalie." Then he perked up. "Maybe you can show me a goalie trick?"

Hank grinned. "Maybe I can."

Jaden reached into his pocket, pulled out an envelope. "Max sent tickets for the team and your family for tomorrow night's game."

Adam snapped those up. "Great. It's really good of you guys to come out. The boys have been excited to meet 'real' hockey players."

"Hey, these kids are the real deal," Hank said. "This is where it all starts."

The men wandered around the rink to the opening, the boys trailing them on the ice.

Elle chewed the inside of her cheek in frustration. And disappointment. She'd really hoped to see Max. To tell him "message received loud and clear." He didn't need to worry about her clinging to him.

She just wanted her underwear back. Because he didn't deserve to have any part of her. Definitely not something as intimate as her panties.

And she wanted to tell him, for Troy's sake, not to be a fool but to take the team's help in dealing with Amber.

Team captain. She'd encouraged him to take the job. And she was happy for him. Only because it benefited the team, of course. It couldn't come at a better time. It would show the team's support of him, their faith in him.

Unfortunately it might all turn sour if Amber continued to play dirty.

Elle's phone signaled a text. From Max:

Couldn't make it to the practice.
Sent Hank and Jaden.

That was it. Nothing personal. She snapped her phone shut. Because that's how it was between them, nothing personal. Spinning on her heels she left the rink.

CHAPTER ELEVEN

ELLE SAT FORWARD in her seat, her eyes glued to the action on the ice, aware of time ticking down. The team needed this win. And it had nothing to do with the fact it was Max's first game as captain.

Hank deflected a shot. Max was there to pick it up and he sent it flying down to Jaden.

"Yeah!" Walter and Adam jumped to their feet along with half the arena.

"Come on, come on," she chanted under her breath, hoping for a clean, hard shot right into the net. Instead it went behind the net. The audience drew in one huge gasp. But Max caught the puck and sent it right back. The goalie was fast. Jaden was faster and the puck sailed into the net setting off the buzzer.

"And the Thunders win!"

The crowd went crazy. Walter's team went wild. Adam and Walter high-fived each other then turned to her. She slapped palms, happy the kids had seen a good game, happy for the team.

And she couldn't help herself, happy for Max. Seemed love didn't just shut off because you willed it to. Which only added frustration to the anger, betrayal, confusion and pain.

"Great game, baby." Hard arms wrapped around her

as Dad swooped her into a bear hug. "Be sure to give Max our thanks."

"I will." He liked notes, perfect.

"Love you." Mom gave Elle a sympathetic look and a squeeze before beginning to shepherd the kids toward the door.

Elle lingered until after the last person left, finally pushing her brother Quinn and his date out the door. Quinn probably wanted to make use of the room. Elle sent him on his way with a scolding shake of her finger.

He grinned, hooked his arm around Valerie's waist and waved goodbye.

Alone, Elle made a sweep around the room, checking to be sure nothing had been left behind. She gathered up a ball cap, a comic book and a pair of sunglasses.

And then she had no reason to stay any longer and she had to admit to herself she'd been hoping Max would come by to say hello to the team.

Stop it, she scolded herself. She was so not a clinger. And she didn't want to be that woman. She refused to be another Amber.

Resolute, she collected her purse, flipped out the lights and went home. Her condo was dark and cold and seemed cramped compared to Max's sprawling home.

She couldn't believe how much she missed Troy.

But she had to put him from her mind.

Her job now was to focus on the Gala, which was just a week away. Refusing to let Max ruin another Christmas and needing to get into the holiday mood, she decided to dig out her Christmas decorations. Thanks to Max and Troy she was way behind in her holiday preparations.

The box she wanted was at the top of the hall closet just out of her reach. She headed for the kitchen for a chair to give her the height she needed, but backtracked when a knock sounded at the door. Probably one of her brothers in search of his sunglasses.

Max stood there, handsome in jeans, a T-shirt and motorcycle jacket. A five-o'clock shadow gave him a sexy air. The bandage on his forehead just added to his rakishness.

Too bad he wasn't hers to unwrap this Christmas. Just looking at him made her ache. He made it so hard to be strong, but she wouldn't be his yo-yo girl.

"Go away, Max. You shouldn't be here." She closed the door but a size-twelve boot stopped her. Then his big body crowded hers in the doorway and she stepped back in sheer self-defense, feeling no shame for the strategic retreat. A girl could only take so much temptation before she melted into a hormonal puddle.

"I made sure no one was around." He followed her step for step until she hard-armed him and he came to a stop. "I needed to see you."

"Why?" As far as she was concerned he'd made it pretty clear he didn't want to see her at all.

He tried to sidestep her restraining hand, but she kept it planted in the middle of his chest. His heartbeat sped up under her palm. Huh. Maybe he wasn't as nonchalant as he appeared.

"How are you?" His hand lifted to her cheek, his fingers a soft caress over the hidden bruise. "I'm sorry you were hurt. I don't think I said that the other night."

"Ray passed on your message."

He cleared his throat. "You have to know it was for the best."

"Do I?"

He scowled. "Amber isn't done making trouble. She's vindictive and now she has you in her sights, too."

"I'm not afraid of Amber."

"Tough cookie." He ran his thumb down the dent of

her chin, amused approval in his midnight-blue eyes. "Nothing scares you."

He scared her. Maybe never finding what she felt for him again scared her. But she wouldn't let fear rule her. She was stronger than that.

Yes, she'd been looking for him to get him to tell her to her face that making love to her had meant nothing to him, to get that measure of respect. But she'd come to her senses. No need to hear the words when his actions spoke so loudly.

So no, he wasn't getting to her again. Crossing her arms in front of herself, she closed herself off from him.

"It's time for you to go."

"I've missed you," he said softly, almost reluctantly. "Troy misses you."

"Why are you here, Max?"

"I shouldn't be. Being with me can only hurt you." He shoved his hands in his pockets as if to contain himself from touching her. "But I couldn't stay away."

"Don't say things you don't mean." Angry, she stomped around him toward the door, determined to send him on his way. "My job is on the line here. Ray instructed me to stay away from you."

He stopped her, taking her hand in his and raising it to his mouth, where he pressed a kiss into her palm. The gesture, his touch, the heat of him down the length of her body, was an intoxicating combination. And oh, how it tempted her, weakened her resolve.

"I hate goodbyes," he whispered against her hair.

He'd told her that before. She remembered feeling sad for him. Now she wondered why he felt compelled to drag this one out.

They were right in front of the open closet door. She caught sight of the box she'd struggled with earlier.

Desperate to change the mood, she twisted away from him and pointed up.

"Before you leave, can you get that box down for me?"

He blinked, obviously thrown off stride by the request.

Good, just as she'd planned—divert his attention and then push him out the door.

He easily palmed the box and drew it down. "Christmas decorations." He sighed as he looked at her. "I should probably think about getting a tree for Troy."

"I'm sure he'd like that." But don't look to her. She was officially done helping him and Troy. And she lied to herself that it was relief she felt, not regret.

Another plan—lie about her feelings until the lie became truth.

She took the box from him, held it between the two of them.

"Deb is with him now. She moved in today."

"Good. That's good." And it was. Both Troy and Max would benefit from her presence in the home.

"Listen, the team is leaving tomorrow for a week of away games. Can you check on Deb while I'm away?"

"Of course." At last, the reason for his visit. Good, now maybe he'd leave. Plus he'd be gone, so she had no problem helping Deb. "Tell her to call me if she needs anything."

"Thanks."

"You'll be back Sunday night, right?"

"No, we had to reschedule a game earlier in the season because of a weather delay flying back from the East Coast. An extra game was added to this series, so we won't be back until Monday."

That's right. She'd intended setting up some additional sponsor visits for the players because they'd be in L.A. on a weekday, but she'd been so wrapped up in Max's business, she hadn't had time.

It was unlike her to let the job suffer. Not that Ray would notice; this was something extra she'd planned to do. But she liked going the extra mile. Taking advantage of opportunities to show sponsor appreciation led to happy sponsors. And happy sponsors made her look good to the owner. She needed to look sharp in order to get the promotion she wanted.

Yeah, she liked that. When she was the PR director, she'd be able to delegate these nuisance personal assignments off to the deputy.

"Congratulations on the win." She changed the subject as she began walking backward toward the door, ignoring the sense that he stalked her. "You guys played great together."

"I took your advice about the captaincy."

"I heard." She bumped into the wooden surface of the door and realized her mistake as he trapped her in place. Only the box prevented him from touching her. "You're already making a difference."

He shook his head. "I liked the way we played tonight, but the win was mostly luck."

"Don't discount your influence."

"I love your optimism."

She froze; his words were too close to the ones she longed to hear. The words she'd never hear from the man who mattered most.

It was too much. Too hard to bear. Ten days ago she'd been strong, heart-whole, career-focused. Here and now that woman was a stranger.

She felt as though she might shatter with her next breath.

"You need to leave."

He nodded but didn't move. "I don't know what this is—was. I wish circumstances were different. I think I'm just broken when it comes to love."

"Nobody said anything about love."

"Babe, your family reeks of it. You deserve the kind of connection your parents have. I'm struggling just to be a good dad."

"You don't have to do it alone."

"I kind of do. You were attacked in my home. Amber is dangerous, and I can't stand the thought of you getting hurt again. It's for your own good."

"Don't tell me that." Pain turning to fury she shoved at him with the box. "Don't make a decision based on your insecurities and tell me it's for my own good. I have two parents and four older brothers I don't let get away with that."

"This is different."

"It's disrespectful, cowardly. I can make my own decisions. And I think I've shown I can take care of myself. If you felt anything for me, you wouldn't let her win."

"You know how I earned the name The Beast?" he asked. "It's because I showed no fear on the ice. I took risks. I fought players bigger and better than me and won because nothing scared me. I lived on the streets, learned to fight where winning meant the difference between life and death. A little squabble over a puck—that was just fun."

"What are you saying?"

"The point is, I had nothing to lose then. But that was before Troy, before you. I can't risk it. I can't risk you. I'm sorry."

"Sorry?" Please.

"Yes. For hurting you. Now, and last year."

She gritted her teeth. This was going from bad to

worse. She told herself to let it go, not to let the past drag her in, but she couldn't help herself.

"You mean at the Gala? When you came on strong and then walked away with someone else? That's what you're sorry for? Or maybe you're sorry for the part where you pretended nothing happened between us?"

"For all of it. I regret anything that hurt you." He met her gaze with complete honesty, making no move to evade her scrutiny. "That night was a fantasy for me. You looked like an angel standing in that doorway. I saw you kiss the others, and I couldn't walk away without a kiss, too."

"It went further than that," she pointed out.

"Yes." He shoved his hands in his pockets. "You tasted so sweet, I just wanted more. The feel of you in my arms brought me alive. I didn't want to give you up. But you had to go back to work, and it was for the best because I came with someone else."

"So you're saying you were playing the gentleman by leaving with the girl you came with?"

He shrugged. "It felt like the right thing to do. I wasn't *with* her, if that's what you think. You ruined me for other women for months."

"Is that why you pretended it never happened?" That's what had really hurt. Being ignored as if the time they spent together meant less than nothing.

He shook his head, his expression fatalistic.

"We had no future. I'd seen you in the stands with your family, knew you'd want more from a relationship than I could give. You were out of my league, and I knew it."

"You are so full of it." Except it fitted with his unexpected humility.

"And the team frowned on players dating staff. You would be the one hurt by that rule, not me. It seemed best to let it end where we left it. It's a memory I cherish."

Even then he'd made decisions for her. And she'd let him. By staying silent, by denying her feelings. Not any-more. All the seething emotions roiling inside her burst out in a raw confession.

"I love you, Max. You're what's best for me. You and Troy. We could have so much more together."

An answering sentiment flared in his eyes, but he quickly shut it down. "The risk to you is too high."

"Shouldn't that be my decision?"

"Not when it's my baggage that will hurt you. I won't be responsible for putting you in Amber's crosshairs. Or causing trouble for your career."

Feeling exposed and rejected, she pulled into herself. "Then there's nothing more to say."

Holding on to her pride, she silently pleaded with him to go, her fingers crumpling the cardboard box where she gripped it, her hold on the box as tight as her hold on her slippery control.

"Except goodbye." He gruffly cleared his throat. "I can't not say goodbye. Not with you."

"Max."

"I came for this." He reached for her over the box, cupped her face and laid his lips on hers.

The kiss was exquisitely tender with a little heat and a lot of promise. The kind of kiss you didn't want to end because you liked where you were. And then it turned a little rough, a whole lot desperate.

Finally he lifted his head and they both fought for air.

He hadn't released her and she felt the struggle in him, the way his body jerked as he fought his instincts when it came to her.

She couldn't look at him, wouldn't watch him leave.

"Goodbye." He pressed a kiss to her bent head. And then he was gone.

* * *

"There. I think that does it." Elle stepped back from the Christmas tree and gave it a once-over. Decked out in glittery snowflakes, hundreds of multicolored miniature lights and playful hockey ornaments, it shimmered in festive glory. "Perfect."

"Oh, my," Deb declared with a laugh. "What fun. I've never thought of doing a themed tree. Where did you find all the little hockey players?"

"From the gift shop at the arena," Elle confessed. "And the plastic pucks and sticks, too. I printed the team pennants on my printer. They add a nice bit of color to the silver and purple bulbs."

"The Thunder colors," Deb observed. "Very clever. Max is going to love it. He doesn't do it for himself, but the year he was with us, he helped me with all the holiday decorating. Oh, he'd complain about being dragged into girl's work, but I could tell he liked the hominess of it."

She turned to take in the rest of the house. Gesturing to the staircase draped in white lights, she said, "You've made the place festive with simple, elegant touches. The use of his team colors is different and brilliant."

Deb spun to Troy.

"What do you think, Troy? Isn't it pretty?"

The boy sat playing in the portable crib they'd placed right in the middle of the living room so he could be a part of the decorating. At the sound of his name he stood and came to the side of the crib.

"Ismas tee," he said, his eyes as bright as the twinkling lights encircling the tree. "Pretty."

He held his arms up to Elle. Now they were finished decorating, she lifted him out, kissed his cheek. He was the reason she was here. She set him on his feet, and he immediately made for the tree.

"Oh, no, you don't." She swept him up again, settled

him on her hip. She smiled at Deb. "From what Max told me, yours was the first place he was in that felt like home."

Deb dropped a box of purple bulbs, causing them to roll all over. "He told you that?" she asked from her knees.

"He really does treasure you." Elle bent to help gather balls and Troy wiggled free and chased after rolling ornaments. She didn't really want to talk about Max but he was Deb's favorite topic.

"Oh dear, I know. I'm surprised he told you. He's a very private man."

"Tell me about it. Getting him to agree to participate in team events is next to impossible. I knew he was a loner, thought it was mostly ego. I was shocked to see how humble he is." She told Deb about the trip to the zoo.

"He's a good man." Deb held the box out for Elle to put her bulbs in. "You should have seen him when he first came to us. He'd been on his own and on the streets for nearly a year. He was closed-mouthed and self-contained, but he soaked up the attention we gave him like sand absorbs water in the desert. It helped that he was the only child with us at the time."

Troy wandered over, took a bulb out of the box so he held one in each hand. Elle ruffled his hair.

"I get the feeling his time on the streets was particularly ugly. He said that's where he learned to fight."

"Yes." Deb nodded. "I channeled all that anger into hockey. It was a perfect fit. I also introduced him to music. He lit up at the piano."

"I've heard him play. He's lucky to have you in his life."

"And I'm lucky to have him in my life. He told me his foundation bought my ranch."

Elle froze. "He has a foundation?"

"Yes, Safe Streets for Kids. He started it when he came back to San Diego. He's planning to build some kind of sports facility. He hasn't gone into any details yet. I'm just thrilled to see the ranch being used for a vital purpose again."

"He really is a special man, isn't he?" Elle had misjudged him right from the beginning. Now she found it all too easy to believe he did everything he could to save kids from the mistakes he'd made. And how like him to keep it all hidden.

Deb took Elle's hands. "And it sounds like he's found someone special in you. I'm so happy for you both."

"No. No, no," Elle quickly corrected her. "We aren't together."

"Oh. That's a shame." Deb squeezed her hands and considered Elle with wise eyes. "You should be."

The Beast Hurt Me And Took My Baby

The headline, along with a picture of a battered Amber, glared out of Elle's laptop.

Sick to her stomach with disgust, she copied the offensive shot and sent it off to Ray and Max, with the tag: the ugly has hit the fan.

Then she dumped the rest of her cereal and raced to get ready for work. Forty minutes later she walked into headquarters and went straight to Ray's office, then diverted to the conference room when she saw that was where the men were gathered.

Hank and Jaden and several other players lingered in the hall outside the conference room. Obviously news had spread quickly.

"Elle." Hank stepped forward. "Tell Max we've got his back."

She nodded, swallowing past the lump in her throat, touched by the team's support of Max. He was so sure he was all alone. And he was so wrong.

She hesitated for a heartbeat when she saw Max sitting there fresh from a winning series on the road. He'd chosen the game over her, but she realized it only made her more determined. Turning the knob, she stepped inside.

All eyes swung to her.

"Elle," Ray spoke first. "I appreciated the early tag this morning, but you were removed from this case."

"I've been involved from the beginning. I can help." Without waiting for permission, she walked around the table and took the only open seat. Right next to Max.

The owner of the team, Carl Carpenter, stood at the front of the room with his hands stuffed into his pockets.

"All assistance is welcome," Carl boomed out in a powerful voice. "Tell me, Ms. Austin, what is your take on the situation?"

"Amber has obviously invented a fraudulent beating to force Max's hand in the custody issue of his son."

Carl pointed to the tabloid resting in the middle of the table. "So you don't think this is real?"

"Someone may have hit her. It wasn't Max."

"You sound very sure."

"I am. Max reserves his violence for the ice rink."

"Max—" Carl switched his attention to her left "—is that true?"

Max shrugged. "I've already told you how we should handle this."

"We are not accepting your resignation." Coach pounded the table. "Get that out of your head. We're finally winning again. I need you. The fans need you. We've been getting positive feedback all week since the article on you and Troy came out in the *Union Tribune*."

"That was before Amber's latest stunt. I knew this would get ugly, but I never conceived of her manufacturing a beating. I'm hurting the team by staying."

"Not you," Elle corrected. "Amber. Has she contacted you?"

"If you count the police on my doorstep at seven this morning as contact, then yeah, I've heard from her." He didn't look at Elle.

She glanced at Ray. "No charges have been made yet."

"And they won't," Coach declared. "Max was in Los Angeles with the team."

"Amber contends he came to her house the night before last, threatened her to leave Troy alone and hit her when she defied him." Ray outlined the official position against Max.

"But the team didn't get back from Los Angeles until last night."

"Exactly," Coach punctuated Elle's protest.

"And we all know he could have driven down after the game and been back in L.A. in a matter of hours." Ray exposed the obvious hole in that defense.

"That's not what happened," Max stated. "So they won't be able to prove it."

Knowing how he disliked explaining himself, Elle fought the urge to show sympathy. She was here for the team, and his resignation was not the answer.

She clasped her hands together, her elbow brushing his suit sleeve.

"We're rehashing information." Carl redirected the conversation. "Our focus needs to be public opinion. We're here to decide what the team can do to help Max."

"I can have a press conference pulled together in two hours," Ray put in. "I think we take the approach that Max was traveling with the team at the time of the alleged assault. That obviously Amber Williams is a disturbed individual, that she was known to leave the child in the care of others for extended periods of time and Max was right to remove his child from her care."

Elle wrote as he spoke, automatically making adjustments as she went.

"Good, but not quite there." Carl began to pace. "Motherhood is a sacred institution. We have to watch our step there. Women, especially single mothers, will identify with her."

"How about this," Elle said then began to read. "'The San Diego Thunder hockey association solidly stands behind their interim captain, Max Beasley, who was traveling with the team at the time of the alleged assault. Max recently learned Ms. Williams was leaving their child in the care of others for extended periods of time and, in the child's best interest, exercised his court-appointed right to assume custody of his son. The team fully expects Max to be cleared of all allegations and supports his decision to protect his child to the best of his ability.'"

"Excellent." Ray nodded at Carl, who nodded back.

"Sir." Elle pushed her luck. "The players want to show their support, too. Perhaps we can have them standing behind Max during the press conference as a show of team solidarity?"

Carl glanced up to the picture windows opening onto the hallway full of Thunder players. He nodded. "Outstanding idea, Elle. Anyone who wants to can participate."

For a brief instant Max squeezed her hand and then released her. She glanced at him, but he was focused on Ray.

"We have a lot of public support, too. Most of what's coming into our social-networking accounts is positive. We want to get our statement out while public opinion is on our side," Ray directed. "Elle, you still need to stay away."

Carl's phone rang and the room went silent as he answered. Elle crossed her fingers.

Carl Carpenter's stoic expression never changed. The call consisted mostly of long silences followed by acknowledging grunts. Finally he thanked the caller and disconnected.

She was aware of Max straightening in his seat, clasping his hands together and leaning forward, ready for the news. Instinctively, she turned to look at him.

"Breathe," he said, even though his attention appeared to be totally on the owner.

"That was my contact at the police department. It's not final, but it's doubtful charges will be brought against Max. They've been unable to find any record of him renting a car on the night in question, and security at the hotel has him going into his room at 11:08 p.m. and not coming out until 8:15 a.m. Plus you signed for room service at 7:37 a.m. The consideration is that your alibi stands up."

A hum of relief went through the room before Ray hopped into action.

"Okay, let's get the statement out to the press and set up the press conference as soon as possible. I want our support of Max known now. Hopefully it'll offset negative speculation. I'll prep Max."

"Thanks for your help, everyone," Carl stated. "Now let's put this one behind us so we can go back to winning games."

CHAPTER TWELVE

YESTERDAY HAD BEEN Max's idea of hell.

Waking up to the police. The meeting at team headquarters with the owner. His life put on display and talked about. Defending himself to the media, to the world.

How he hated being in the limelight.

Most of all he hated Amber. She'd gone too far this time. Faking a beating, bringing him up on assault charges, was unforgivable. He wanted her out of his life. More, he wanted her out of Troy's life.

Well, it ended here. Ended now.

Finding the address he sought, he parked and walked into the building. The colorful decorations and blooming poinsettia plants made him think of Elle. She'd turned his house into a glittering winter wonderland complete with a hockey-themed Christmas tree.

Being on his own, he'd never bothered to get a tree. This was his first. Decorated specifically for him. Sentimental sap that he was, he loved it.

He liked all the festive touches throughout the entire house. And when he'd found out Elle was responsible for most of it, he liked it even more.

Until that moment, his house had simply been the place he currently lived in. Elle's personal touches of Christmas magic gave him the best present ever. She'd given him a home.

He came to a sudden stop in the middle of the lobby.

It wasn't the tree at all. He loved Elle.

Life immediately shifted into place. Hope rose in him as the general sense of dissatisfaction he'd been living under disappeared. The past few days had been a revelation to him. The way the team supported him in the face of Amber's lies, the players standing up with him as he addressed the public, hearing Donna take his side over her daughter's on the TV news had all been powerful moments.

The biggest thrill came from hearing Elle champion him. Her show of faith in him moved him to his core. That was love.

Acknowledging the emotion made him realize she was the real reason he was here. His home wouldn't be complete until she shared it with him.

He moved forward with purpose.

Moments later he was face-to-face with his nemesis. Amber sat back in a black leather barrel chair flirting with his investigator, Kit Peters. Any evidence of her supposed assault was hidden behind an artful makeup job and oversize sunglasses.

Just the sight of her turned his stomach.

"Hey, lover." Satisfaction dripped from her drawled greeting. "Ready to talk to me now?"

Max ignored her. His attorney Harold Jones stood by the window. Max nodded to him before addressing Kit. "Are you taping?"

"Yes. Have a seat and we'll get started."

Max shook his head. He preferred to stand.

"Taping?" Amber straightened in her seat, suddenly a little less blasé. "There will be no taping."

"I told you to bring your attorney."

"I can handle myself."

"Right. More likely he dumped you after your allegations against me were proven false."

"I warned you I would fight for Troy."

"You don't want him. You just want the income that comes with him."

"I deserve it. It's hard work raising a kid."

"Except Donna has been the one raising him. You know how I know? He's asked about Donna and spoken to her every day. He hasn't asked for you."

"That doesn't mean anything."

"It means everything to me. And if you'd been successful in getting me convicted of assault, I'd be in jail and you'd be gallivanting around again. Troy would have no one. I'm never going to let that happen.

"This meeting is a bust." Max glanced at Kit and Harold. "Thanks. Sorry to waste your time." He turned to leave.

"Hey," she protested. "You can't leave. We just got started."

"You're a liar, a cheat and a fraud. No taping. No lawyer. No discussion. Kit, give the photos to the police."

"Wait." Amber jumped to her feet. "What photos?"

Max kept going.

"I said wait." She followed him to the door. But he wasn't playing. "Okay, you can tape the conversation."

Tempted to walk on and leave her to her fate, he gritted his teeth and made himself backtrack. He needed her signature on that document.

Because he wanted Elle to be the mother of his children.

Back in the office, Max looked at Kit and received a nod. They were taping.

"I don't know what the big deal is." Amber went back to her seat.

"This conversation is going to be very short and mostly one-sided. I want you out of my son's life—"

"I told you what it would take." Smug again, she crossed her legs.

Skinny legs. He ran his gaze over her, noting the bottle-blond hair and heavy makeup that didn't quite hide the hard lines around her mouth. What had he ever seen in her?

"I've always known I could buy you off, but I never wanted to have to tell Troy you cared so little for him you sold off your rights. I don't care anymore. Better that conversation than let you destroy his childhood. So, this is how it's going to be. I give you a hundred thousand dollars, and you sign over your rights to Troy. And then you're going to move to another state and never come near us again."

She cocked her head. "I think you're missing a zero in that number."

"Show her the pictures," he directed Kit.

Amber's haughty expression was belied by the shake in her hand as she took the manila folder the investigator passed across the desk. Her arrogance disappeared along with the color in her face as she shuffled through the pile.

"You bastard," she accused him. "You had me followed. You had no right. Some of these are in Phoenix." As if that made a difference.

"You left our child with a stranger," he bit out. "I have every right to protect him in any way I see fit."

"She wasn't a stranger to me."

"Another lie. We have a deposition. You knew her for two weeks. You had no idea what she might do with him." He wanted this done. "Sign the document."

She stuck her pointed chin in the air. "Add a zero."

"You just lost five thousand."

She blinked and angry color mottled her cheeks. "You can't do that."

"It's now ninety. Harold, tell her what happens if the photos go to the police."

"The punishment for child neglect or abandonment can be imprisonment for up to one year. More if there are circumstances such as drug use that expose a child to further harm."

"I never—"

"Don't even bother." Max plucked a picture out of her hand, held it up for her to see and tossed it onto the desk. "Sign the release while I'm still feeling generous."

"This is because of *her,* isn't it?"

"She has nothing to do with this." He hated to hear her mention Elle. "You abandoned our child. You tried to have me arrested. This is all *your* doing. There's enough here to ensure you'll never see Troy alone again. Take the money and move to Las Vegas with Donna or, hell, move to Phoenix. I don't care."

"You are such an ass," she yelled. "You can have him. All he does is scream. I never wanted a kid. This was just supposed to be a quick way to get a lot of money. So pay up and I'm out of here. And a measly hundred grand isn't going to do it."

There it was—confirmation she'd set him up.

He waited for the familiar rage to rush through his blood, but it didn't come. He couldn't find regret in him anywhere.

He loved Troy, couldn't imagine life without him. She'd given Max an irreplaceable, priceless gift and she didn't even know it. Their son was a meal ticket to her and that sealed the deal for him.

If she changed her ways in the future and sincerely decided she wanted to be a part of Troy's life, Max might relent, but he refused to give her leverage to jerk Troy's emotions around for financial gain.

No rights meant she had nothing to bargain with. And if she thought she could come along later and threaten to make Max out as the bad guy, he had the tape of today's meeting, so Troy could hear exactly what really happened.

"Good, because it's down to eighty thousand." Amber shrieked and Max realized where Troy got his penchant for screaming. He'd heard enough.

"I'm giving you a chance to change your life. I encourage you to take it." Max pushed away from the wall. He waved to Kit. "Harold, the deal is off the table in ten minutes."

"You bas—" The door closed off the obscenity. And that quickly, a chapter in his life ended.

His son was as safe as Max could make him. Now, he just needed to convince Elle that she belonged with the two of them.

San Diego embraced Christmas. Lights decorated houses, yards, boats and freeways. The malls decked their halls with boughs of holly, marching soldiers and oversize glittering snowflakes while Santa's helpers collected donations, listened attentively to childish desires and smiled prettily for the camera.

Elle loved the season, loved watching the boats gaily parade along the embarcadero, the Grinch's heart triple in size at The Old Globe theater and Marines collect toys for tots.

But now none of it held Elle's attention or pulled her from the funk she'd fallen into.

Not even the magic of Christmas and shopping for

friends and family cheered her up. And she loved to Christmas-shop, had even taken on the task of buying gifts for the team. What was better than shopping with someone else's money? Not so fun this year.

What really made her mad was on top of all the emotional angst he'd put her through, this made two years in a row Max had spoiled her Christmas.

Not that she let it show through her determinedly in-the-season jolliness.

Elle held up two dresses for Amanda and Michelle to see. "The black or the green?"

"Green," they both answered at once.

"It looks great with your hair," Michelle raved.

"And your skin. I've always been jealous that you have fewer freckles than me," Amanda lamented. "Life is not fair."

Michelle rolled her eyes. A tall, lithe strawberry-blonde, Amanda radiated wholesome beauty. "You're gorgeous, so don't worry about it."

"I'm so glad you could both come to the Gala. And that you could come a day early to shop for a dress," Elle told her best friends. Choked up, she blinked back tears. She was so happy to have them here. She really needed their help.

"How could we refuse? When we heard the highly organized, always-three-steps-ahead-of-the-rest-of-the-world Elle Austin hadn't bought her dress for her team's big gala, we knew it was an emergency." Michelle's warm hug took the sting out of her words. "Did I tell you Gabe is coming, too? He's flying into San Diego tomorrow morning. You'll both get to meet him."

"That's great. I'm so happy for you." Elle cringed at how lacking in sincerity that sounded. "Sorry. I really do mean it."

"Girlfriend, I get it. It's hard to see someone in love when you're hurting."

"Max makes me so furious," Elle vented. "How I hate being held back for 'my own good.'"

"You know your family does it because they care and want to protect you," Amanda pointed out.

"I know. They don't see how demeaning it is. It's like they want to prevent me from participating in my own life. There are times I'd like to protect them, too, but I draw the line at making decisions for them."

"It may be frustrating, but at least they care enough to get involved. When I lived with my grandparents I often felt like a spectator. I'm so glad to finally have my own place."

"Are you trying to say I'm spoiled?" Elle asked with wry humor. "Believe me, I know I'm lucky to have such a loving family. But let me tell you, there are times when it's possible to have too much of a good thing. For Max to do the same thing is too much."

"You do know what that means, right?" Michelle didn't look up from the silver lamé mini she'd pulled from the rack.

"What it means?" Elle carried both the black and the green gown toward the dressing room.

"Yeah." Michelle followed with the silver lamé. "Max loves you."

Elle froze, causing Michelle to run into her. "What?"

"Isn't it obvious? Your family wants to protect you for your own good because they love you. Max is doing the same thing."

"She's right," Amanda agreed. "You were attacked in his house. By the mother of his child. She's in his life to stay. What could he do besides push you away?"

"Max is an emotionally stunted man afraid to risk happiness for fear of being abandoned again." Okay, no bitterness in that comment.

"And then there's that." Amanda nodded.

Elle rolled her eyes and escaped into the dressing cubicle. Once inside she stripped out of her jeans and sweater and pulled on the green dress, but that's as far as she got. Fighting tears she laid her forehead on the cool glass of the mirror.

How could they take his side? They were her friends. They were supposed to take her side no matter what.

Didn't they understand she didn't need protection? She needed the man she loved to love her back. To trust her to help him, to be strong for him.

She needed him to fight for her.

She knew he cared for her. His goodbye kiss, so full of tenderness and regret, told her that. But not enough. He certainly didn't love her.

Maybe she deserved the heartache. How arrogant of her to think she could set limits on love, keep her emotions in a neat and tidy box, order her perfect man as if he were an item on a menu. Less sports, more arts, tall, dark and handsome. Check. Check. Check.

Only problem was he didn't love her back. Just one of life's little jokes. And it was on her.

"Oh, babe." Warm arms wrapped around her and suddenly Amanda and Michelle were there squeezing into the small room and the three of them were crushed together holding each other.

They crowded onto the small bench and Elle poured her heart out. They gave her the love and sympathy she craved. Finally she dried her eyes. Pulling her pride around herself, she blew her nose.

"He doesn't know what he's missing," she announced.

Standing, she presented her back to Amanda. "Zip me, please."

Her friend complied and Elle turned to check out her reflection. She frowned; the color was nice but the fit was loose. She'd lost weight over the past week.

Michelle had been tapping her lip, her gaze contemplative.

"What?" Elle asked, knowing that look.

"I think you should show him—" she smiled maliciously "—exactly what he's missing."

"Hmm." Elle cocked her head and pondered her reflection. "You're right," she said, feeling her resilience rebounding. How could she expect him to fight for them if she wasn't willing to do the same? "This dress won't do at all. I need something with less material." She met Michelle's evil grin with one of her own. "Something sexy."

The day of the San Diego Thunder's Wish upon a Puck Gala dawned gray and drizzly. Elle's whole day was dedicated to the event, so Ray had approved the expenditure of a guest room for her at the event hotel, the tropical resort of Paradise Pointe on Mission Bay.

After a breakfast of oatmeal with cranberries and bananas, she grabbed her overnight case and her garment bag with her sexy dress and headed to Mission Bay. A lot of the guests had chosen to stay over at the hotel, including Michelle and Amanda and Elle's parents.

The Gala started at eight. Her schedule had her dressed and at the event by seven to oversee the final touches and the arrival of the guests. Her girls planned to meet her at five-thirty to help her dress.

Time flew by. Elle worked with a team, including Jenna, who kept her apprised of catering, auction, guests and VIPs. A thousand dollars a plate earned the attendee a gourmet dinner, a huge gift basket, an opportunity to spend more money on great auction items and an extravagant event hobnobbing with VIPs, celebrities and the Thunder team.

It was the place to be in San Diego tonight.

Max called her twice during the day. Heart racing, she rejected the calls. Tempted as she was to talk to him, she didn't dare allow him to interfere with her concentration. Not today.

Michelle stopped by and introduced her fiancé, Gabe, a tall, quiet man who looked at her friend with solemn devotion. They were on their way out to drop their ward, Jack, off at Adam and Stephanie's.

"It's so great of your family to take him tonight."

"Are you kidding? Stephanie is thrilled. She's been making noises about having another baby. I think Adam is hoping watching Jack will cure her of the notion."

"Uh-oh." Michelle exchanged glances with Gabe. "That might backfire on him. Jack is a really good baby."

Elle shrugged and grinned. "Then I'll have another niece or nephew. You guys have fun tonight."

"We will." Michelle reached for Gabe's hand. "Jack is a great baby, but it'll still be good to have Gabe to myself. I plan to do lascivious things to his prime body."

"Hussy."

"Hey," Gabe protested. "I'm hoping we'll be friends. No discouraging her."

Elle laughed and kissed his cheek. "My friend, that *was* encouragement." She moved over and hugged Michelle and Jack. "Ravish away," she whispered. "He's a keeper."

"He is." Michelle nodded. "I'll be back to help you dress so you can snag your guy." With a wave they left and Elle went back to work.

Once the event started, she'd be able to hand her duties off to Ray. Jenna would be helping with the auction so Elle would be free to shift her attention to her future and wowing Max.

Management was a little worried that Max's recent appearance in the tabloids might affect the turnout, so Elle made a point of touching base with managers, assistants, agents and publicists throughout the day.

"Nobody seems to be shying away," she happily informed Ray when he called at five.

"Excellent." His relief came clearly through the line. "Carl will be comforted to hear that. Max, too. How is Natalie doing?"

"Fine." The owner's daughter had arrived fifteen minutes ago and had already second-guessed several of her original decisions, which Elle had been seeing put into place all day. "She's a little nervous, but it's going to be a beautiful event."

"Don't let her change anything," he instructed, obviously familiar with Natalie's mercurial habits. "Hold her hand and keep her out of trouble until I get there."

"Okay," she agreed and hung up. "Except how to do that?" she muttered, since it was time for her to head upstairs to get dressed. If Elle could trust Natalie not to undo everything they'd done today, she'd prefer to leave the socialite in charge. But she couldn't risk the woman wreaking havoc in Elle's absence.

She joined Natalie and Jenna at the gift-basket table. Jenna had already changed so she could cover for Elle. Elle noticed Natalie wasn't ready and decided to suggest this lull before the storm as the best time for both of them to be away.

"Are you sure?" Natalie asked. "I was going to wait until closer to six or six-thirty."

"It's really slowed down here at the welcome table. I think it's safe to slip away now. I don't expect attendees to start arriving at the ballroom until close to seven-thirty, but I want to be ready early just in case."

"Good idea," Natalie agreed. "It always seems to take longer to get ready than I think it will." She waved and took off for the elevators.

Elle sighed in relief and turned to Jenna. "Stick to her like glue if she gets to the ballroom before me."

"Will do," Jenna agreed with a meaningful nod.

Elle thanked her and escaped to her room. She quickly showered and smoothed on lotion. A knock sounded on the door and she opened it to Michelle and Amanda.

"Come in." She grinned at them. "Time to make me beautiful. I can't wait to see Max's face when he spies me in the dress."

"Me, too," they chimed.

Amanda held up a curling iron. "Let's get to work."

CHAPTER THIRTEEN

MAX FOUND A CORNER and planted himself against the wall. He'd had enough notoriety to last a lifetime and he planned to keep a low profile tonight. And yet people still found him, many coming up to wish him well either with the team, which was continuing to win, or with Troy.

It was a little disconcerting.

But he took it in his stride even as he plotted to grab Elle and steal her away as soon as possible. He missed her so much. He just wanted to talk to her, to explain where his head had been and tell her he loved her.

Okay, if he were being honest, that last thing nearly had him hyperventilating. But he put on his game face and reminded himself he was playing this one for life.

He'd been alone for so long he'd come to think of himself as a loner. These past few days had shown him how wrong he was. He had a family, not only Troy and Deb, but the whole Thunder team.

He just needed Elle to give it all meaning.

Several times he caught a glimpse of her in the crowd. In the end that's what drew him from his corner, the necessity to find her and make her his.

And then the crowd parted and he saw her. She stole his breath.

Yellow silk wrapped her body as faithfully as sunshine,

beautifully showcasing the pale perfection of her bare shoulders and subtle hint of cleavage. Her dark auburn hair flowed over one bare shoulder in cascading curls and her pretty brown eyes were shadowed in smoky layers, giving her a sultry look.

Sexy, radiant, gorgeous. She made his mouth water, his mind reel and his heart ache.

He stalked her, not a difficult task since she came straight for him. They met in the middle of the dance floor just as music swelled and people began to crowd around them.

He held his hand out to her and she took it. Pulling her close, he wrapped her in his arms and moved slowly to the music. He sighed. This felt so right.

Elle settled against him with a sigh of her own. It seemed so long since she'd been in his arms and she'd missed the sense of belonging. She allowed herself only a moment to savor his closeness before putting a little steel in her spine and pulling back.

"How is Troy?" she asked.

"He misses you."

"I miss him, too." The little guy had really wrapped himself around her heart. "What are you going to do about it?"

"I've been trying to reach you."

Not exactly the response she'd been looking for. "I'm sorry I missed your calls today. I was busy with the event."

"I wanted to let you know Amber is gone."

Elle tripped over his feet. "What?"

"She signed her rights over to me and left town."

"Why?" Shocked, she tried to make sense of his revelation. Amber was gone.

"Because Troy and I deserve a fresh start and we

wouldn't get it with her dragging us down. Because she hurt you, and nobody gets away with that in front of me."

"Max." She didn't know what to say. She never expected this.

"And that includes me. You were right." He leaned his chin on her temple as if unable to look at her as he made his confession. "I was a coward for not acting on my feelings for you."

"Your feelings?" She held her breath. Was it going to be this easy? His expression when he saw her across the room had been everything she'd hoped for. He'd practically drooled. A highly satisfying moment. And she'd almost missed it because she'd been drooling over him, too.

His tux showcased his broad shoulders, and the blindingly white pleated shirt offset his tanned skin perfectly. He looked strong and healthy and fit. And she'd been more than ready to confront him and demand he deal with her.

Now she thought about it, he'd already been on his way toward her.

"I love you, Elle."

Her throat closed as emotion overwhelmed her. She had started the night thinking she needed to fight for his love, but he'd beat her to it, freely admitting his feeling for her.

"Oh, Max." She framed his face and made him look at her. "Truly?"

And there it was in his eyes, the regret, the pain, the hope, the love, all laid bare for her to see.

"I love you, too." She breathed against his mouth, allowing herself to believe this moment was really happening.

She suddenly realized there was a hush in the room and she and Max lifted their heads to see the music had stopped and they were the only ones left standing in the middle of the deserted dance floor. Ray stood at the podium ready to start the program.

Elle felt heat flood her cheeks and she pulled on Max's hand. Not only did she want out of the spotlight, she longed to get him alone to finish their discussion.

But Max had other ideas. He held up a hand to Ray. "I'm going to need a minute here." And he went down on one knee.

"Oh my God. Max." Elle tugged on his hand. The room blared with silence around them.

He didn't fight her, but he didn't rise either. He clasped both her hands in his and offered her his soul.

"I love you, Elle Austin." The words were for her alone, but he didn't seem to care who heard them. "I'm a better man when I'm with you. A better father. You've shown me what it means to be a family, but I need you to make it complete. Will you marry me?"

No longer caring about the crowd, Elle sank to her knees along with him. This was everything she yearned for but hadn't dreamed was within her grasp.

"For Troy's sake?" she asked.

He nodded and her heart sank a little. She shouldn't have asked. Because she almost didn't care.

"This whole debacle with Amber made one thing clear to me. I want you to be the mother of my children. So yes, for Troy, but mostly for me."

Tears threatened to fall as her heart swelled with love. Looking into his eyes, seeing adoration gazing back at her, lifted her to the height of angels. Sportsman, pianist, philanthropist: she loved all parts of him.

"I need you in my life. And I want it to be forever. Say yes." He jerked his head toward the crowd. "Soon, please."

"I've missed you and Troy so very much. My life has been so dull and orderly without you. I need the color and chaos you bring. I love you more than I believed possible. And my family is really big on love."

She threw her arms around his neck and put him out of his misery. "Yes, please."

Applause broke out.

"Excellent." He kissed her hard, and standing, he swooped her up in his arms and carried her off.

"Congratulations to Max and Elle." Ray took control of the program. "Ladies and gentlemen, it looks like Max got the best prize of the evening, but we have lots of wonderful items to auction off. This is a good opportunity to announce that the San Diego Thunder organization will be partnering with Max Beasley's foundation, Safe Streets for Kids, in building a sports camp for kids in east San Diego. It'll have an ice rink and soccer fields..."

Elle stopped listening. Max loved her. He'd just claimed her in front of his entire team and her friends and family.

She leaned forward and kissed his jaw, claiming him, too.

Showing the world they were a team.

A whisper came to her from the crowd. "They're perfect together. It's like watching *Beauty and the Beast.*"

Elle stared into Max's eyes. Yeah, she could live with that.

A week later Elle sat cross-legged in the middle of Max's bed putting the finishing touches on his gift. She fussed with the white bow on the red-wrapped package, anxious for Max to finish his shower.

It was five after midnight and she couldn't wait to start their first Christmas together. She had several gifts for him actually, including the sexy nightie she wore under his shirt.

They'd just finished putting Troy's gifts under the tree,

including a wagon and a tricycle Max had had to put together. She'd always loved Christmas but this year, with her own family, she felt the magic more than ever as she overflowed with happiness.

The day was completely planned out. Up early to open gifts. She couldn't wait to see Troy's face when he saw the gift-shrouded Christmas tree. Elle insisted that Deb spend Christmas with them and the older woman would be making breakfast and then they were all headed to church with her family followed by holiday festivities and dinner at her folks' house.

A wonderful day that she truly looked forward to, but first she wanted this time with the love of her life. She heard the shower turn off and her heart raced in anticipation.

He was so good to her, he had even sat through a viewing of *Beauty and the Beast.* She'd heard the comment so often she'd decided he needed to share the joke. He'd been very good-natured about it; of course that could be due to the sensual bribe she'd given him.

He strolled in, wrapped in a towel, his hair still damp from the shower, his broad shoulders gleaming in the bedside light.

Oh yeah, she was ready to pay up again right now.

He lay down beside her and yanked on a strand of her hair. "What did Ray have to say?"

The team offices had been on vacation since the day after the Gala, so she hadn't heard how they were taking her relationship with Max.

"He said I can keep my job. It seems management has a problem with staff dating players, but a committed relationship is okay."

"I'm glad." He kissed her softly. "I didn't want your career to suffer because of me."

"It would have been worth it," she assured him, and then she grinned. "I would have hit you up for a job with the foundation."

"And I would have given you one. But I know you've been working hard for the directorship."

"I'm going to get it, too."

"I don't doubt it." He ran a finger down her arm. "I'm glad Deb took the job with the foundation. She'll be the perfect manager for the sports camp. She gets to stay on her family land, but with a property manager on-site she won't be alone."

"She was so excited she was in tears. It was the best Christmas present you could give her."

"Talking about Christmas presents." He flicked the bow on the red package. "Is this for me?"

Suddenly uncertain, she hesitated before setting it in front of him. "Yes. I hope you like it."

He looked at her a long time and then plucked the bow off. A moment later he revealed a scarlet crystal rose.

She bit her lip waiting for him to react. He gave nothing away as he stared at the eight-inch, long-stemmed rose.

"I know, it's silly. It means—"

"Shh." He pressed a finger to her lips. He carefully set the rose on the bedside table and tossed the box aside before pinning her to the bed. "It's The Beast's rose, full of love that will never wilt." He kissed her forehead. "Never fade." His lips whispered over her cheek. "Never die." His mouth adored hers in simple caresses that deepened and grew, relentlessly arousing her passion up until her nerves tingled and her muscles melted. "I get it. Best of all I get you."

He lifted his head and the look in his eyes revealed she'd touched something primal in him. "I love you so much. And you deserve soft words and gentle caresses. But it's all I can do not to ravish you."

"Oh, goody." She released the button holding his shirt together and it fell open showing him her sheer nightie. Then she looped her arms around his head. "There is a Santa Claus."

* * * * *

Mills & Boon® Hardback

December 2012

ROMANCE

A Ring to Secure His Heir	Lynne Graham
What His Money Can't Hide	Maggie Cox
Woman in a Sheikh's World	Sarah Morgan
At Dante's Service	Chantelle Shaw
At His Majesty's Request	Maisey Yates
Breaking the Greek's Rules	Anne McAllister
The Ruthless Caleb Wilde	Sandra Marton
The Price of Success	Maya Blake
The Man From her Wayward Past	Susan Stephens
Blame it on the Bikini	Natalie Anderson
The English Lord's Secret Son	Margaret Way
The Secret That Changed Everything	Lucy Gordon
Baby Under the Christmas Tree	Teresa Carpenter
The Cattleman's Special Delivery	Barbara Hannay
Secrets of the Rich & Famous	Charlotte Phillips
Her Man In Manhattan	Trish Wylie
His Bride in Paradise	Joanna Neil
Christmas Where She Belongs	Meredith Webber

MEDICAL

From Christmas to Eternity	Caroline Anderson
Her Little Spanish Secret	Laura Iding
Christmas with Dr Delicious	Sue MacKay
One Night That Changed Everything	Tina Beckett

Mills & Boon® Large Print
December 2012

ROMANCE

Contract with Consequences	Miranda Lee
The Sheikh's Last Gamble	Trish Morey
The Man She Shouldn't Crave	Lucy Ellis
The Girl He'd Overlooked	Cathy Williams
Mr Right, Next Door!	Barbara Wallace
The Cowboy Comes Home	Patricia Thayer
The Rancher's Housekeeper	Rebecca Winters
Her Outback Rescuer	Marion Lennox
A Tainted Beauty	Sharon Kendrick
One Night With The Enemy	Abby Green
The Dangerous Jacob Wilde	Sandra Marton

HISTORICAL

A Not So Respectable Gentleman?	Diane Gaston
Outrageous Confessions of Lady Deborah	Marguerite Kaye
His Unsuitable Viscountess	Michelle Styles
Lady with the Devil's Scar	Sophia James
Betrothed to the Barbarian	Carol Townend

MEDICAL

Sydney Harbour Hospital: Bella's Wishlist	Emily Forbes
Doctor's Mile-High Fling	Tina Beckett
Hers For One Night Only?	Carol Marinelli
Unlocking the Surgeon's Heart	Jessica Matthews
Marriage Miracle in Swallowbrook	Abigail Gordon
Celebrity in Braxton Falls	Judy Campbell

Mills & Boon® Hardback

January 2013

ROMANCE

Beholden to the Throne	Carol Marinelli
The Petrelli Heir	Kim Lawrence
Her Little White Lie	Maisey Yates
Her Shameful Secret	Susanna Carr
The Incorrigible Playboy	Emma Darcy
No Longer Forbidden?	Dani Collins
The Enigmatic Greek	Catherine George
The Night That Started It All	Anna Cleary
The Secret Wedding Dress	Ally Blake
Driving Her Crazy	Amy Andrews
The Heir's Proposal	Raye Morgan
The Soldier's Sweetheart	Soraya Lane
The Billionaire's Fair Lady	Barbara Wallace
A Bride for the Maverick Millionaire	Marion Lennox
Take One Arranged Marriage...	Shoma Narayanan
Wild About the Man	Joss Wood
Breaking the Playboy's Rules	Emily Forbes
Hot-Shot Doc Comes to Town	Susan Carlisle

MEDICAL

The Surgeon's Doorstep Baby	Marion Lennox
Dare She Dream of Forever?	Lucy Clark
Craving Her Soldier's Touch	Wendy S. Marcus
Secrets of a Shy Socialite	Wendy S. Marcus

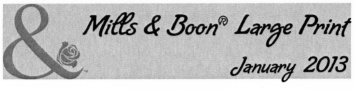

Mills & Boon® Large Print

January 2013

ROMANCE

Unlocking her Innocence	Lynne Graham
Santiago's Command	Kim Lawrence
His Reputation Precedes Him	Carole Mortimer
The Price of Retribution	Sara Craven
The Valtieri Baby	Caroline Anderson
Slow Dance with the Sheriff	Nikki Logan
Bella's Impossible Boss	Michelle Douglas
The Tycoon's Secret Daughter	Susan Meier
Just One Last Night	Helen Brooks
The Greek's Acquisition	Chantelle Shaw
The Husband She Never Knew	Kate Hewitt

HISTORICAL

His Mask of Retribution	Margaret McPhee
How to Disgrace a Lady	Bronwyn Scott
The Captain's Courtesan	Lucy Ashford
Man Behind the Façade	June Francis
The Highlander's Stolen Touch	Terri Brisbin

MEDICAL

Sydney Harbour Hospital: Marco's Temptation	Fiona McArthur
Waking Up With His Runaway Bride	Louisa George
The Legendary Playboy Surgeon	Alison Roberts
Falling for Her Impossible Boss	Alison Roberts
Letting Go With Dr Rodriguez	Fiona Lowe
Dr Tall, Dark...and Dangerous?	Lynne Marshall